BEYOND THE SUNSET AND STARS

PRITOM BARMAN

For those who believe in love beyond the ordinary, and the magic of second chances

Contents

Foreword

When I first introduced Gaurav, Prakriti, and Hardy to the world, I never anticipated the love and connection they'd inspire. *Beneath the Sunset and Stars* was, at its core, a story of finding love in the most unexpected ways, yet *Beyond the Sunset and Stars* seeks to explore what happens after those first magical moments. It dives into the hurdles, the surprises, and yes, the messes that life brings even after love is found. Gaurav and Prakriti's journey is far from over, and as they face new challenges, I hope this sequel provides you with the same comfort and joy you found in the first book.

This story grew from my love for the characters and the world they inhabit—and from the encouragement and enthusiasm of readers like you. For those of you returning, welcome back to Gaurav and Prakriti's world. And to the new readers, here's hoping you find a piece of yourself in these pages.

Preface

What comes after the happily ever after? For Gaurav and Prakriti, love didn't solve every problem; it simply opened the door to new ones. In *Beyond the Sunset and Stars*, I wanted to explore love that persists in the face of change, misunderstanding, and rivalry. I wanted to take Gaurav and Prakriti beyond their sunset and into the unknown, where reality sometimes bends, and where everyday life mingles with the extraordinary.

Expect laughter, arguments, and perhaps a bit of magical realism as Gaurav and Prakriti navigate the next chapter of their story. Alongside them is Hardy, the wise turtle, and a new furry friend who's sure to bring some chaos into the mix. This story invites you to reflect on how love can be both grounding and transformative, and how sometimes, it's the journey after we find love that truly shapes us.

Acknowledgements

This book would not have come to life without the support, encouragement, and belief of so many incredible people.

To my readers, thank you for the messages, reviews, and unwavering support for Gaurav and Prakriti's story. Your excitement kept me inspired even during moments of writer's block.

To my family and friends, thank you for your patience as I disappeared into the world of this story once again. For the late-night brainstorming sessions and endless cups of coffee, I am so grateful.

A special thank you to those who took the time to dive into drafts and give feedback. You each helped this story find its way.

And finally, to Gaurav, Prakriti, Hardy, and now Destroyer—thank you for being the voices in my head that refuse to stay silent. You remind me every day why I love this craft.

Prologue

Well, well, well... Look who's back! Or maybe this is your first time here? Either way, welcome. If you survived *Beneath the Sunset and Stars* and still came back for round two, consider this my official thank-you—and, let's be real, a bit of an apology. After all, you voluntarily re-entered my chaotic life, and for that, I commend you. Seriously, your support means a lot... even if my creator (a.k.a. unosriptom) has this strange habit of sprinkling my life with unexpected, sometimes absurd, twists.

If you're new here, you might be wondering why we're calling this a 'sequel.' My advice? You've got some catching up to do. Go grab *Beneath the Sunset and Stars* on Amazon (yes, I'm shamelessly promoting it—unosriptom won't mind), and dive into the backstory. In that roller-coaster of a book, I, Gaurav—a caffeine-dependent, slightly cynical software developer—was living my predictable, slightly mundane life when Prakriti entered. Or should I say Dr. Prakriti? Yep, she's the kind of smart that makes me feel like I'm back in high school, struggling with calculus.

Anyway, long story short: there I was, coding my way through the world, and Prakriti showed up, reminding me that there's more to life than debugging software. She's got wit, charm, and a kind of beauty that even my dry sense of humor can't fully capture. The universe (and unosriptom) thought it'd be fun to throw us together, and, well, let's just say things got interesting. Oh, and I can't forget our third 'unofficial roommate'—Hardy, my pet turtle, who is basically the Napoleon of turtles. He spends his days in his tank, plotting world domination and splashing water every time he's not the center of attention.

So here we are. Welcome to round two, the next chapter in my ongoing saga, where I dive headfirst into love, life, and whatever else unosriptom has planned for me. Let's hope he doesn't bend my life too far off-course this time. Although, knowing him, that's wishful thinking. And if you're wondering, yes, there will be a lot of rom-com-style chaos, courtesy of yours truly.

So sit back, grab your coffee, and hold on tight. It's a rom-com, after all, and I'm 95% sure unosriptom won't let me fall too hard. But just in case... keep the hope alive. And if you need a recap, think again—jump right into *Beneath the Sunset and Stars* for the whole story. Ready? Here's to love, laughter, and whatever else life has waiting for us. Let's roll!

Note from the Writer: *Hey there, reader! Thanks for joining us on this wild ride once again. If you're new here, welcome—and if you're back for the sequel, well, I hope you're ready. Writing Beneath the Sunset and Stars was just as much of a roller-coaster for me as it was for Gaurav (don't let him fool you, he secretly enjoyed it). I'd say I'm here to make his life easier this time around, but where's the fun in that? Besides, I think he's handling things just fine... mostly.*

Gaurav might not always appreciate my creative liberties—apparently, he's a fan of "keeping things simple." But hey, what's a rom-com without a few detours, right? And let's be honest: with Prakriti (sorry, Dr. Prakriti) and Hardy the turtle, it's never going to be a dull moment. So, grab a coffee, settle in, and let's dive into another round of unpredictable twists, unlikely romance, and a hint of turtle-driven chaos. Enjoy the journey, folks!

1
The First Spark and The Final Ride

So here we are, right back where it all began—the café where I first saw her. Yes, Prakriti, my soulmate, the love of my life, and the reason I'm here telling this story yet again. And no, this café still isn't sponsoring me (maybe they'll reconsider someday?). Just a hint for anyone trying to spot it: it's a cozy spot filled with books...lots of them.

I take her hand, the ring I gave her catching a soft glow from the café's warm lighting. "The first time I saw you right here," I say, trying to sound cool and romantic all at once.

She raises an eyebrow with a smirk. "What if I wasn't here that day?" she asks, a mischievous glint in her eyes. "Would you have just found someone else?"

Ah, one of *those* questions. The kind that only has two possible answers: the right one, or the one that gets you a disapproving look and possibly a month's worth of awkward silences. My mind races through all the possible responses.

I decide to laugh it off. "Just pulling your leg, Gaurav," she grins, giving my hand a squeeze. "I just feel so lucky to be here with you...and, of course, Hardy." Yes, even on date nights, our turtle gets his share of the spotlight. Apparently, he's the most significant third wheel in rom-com history.

Then she gets this dreamy look in her eyes and sighs, "It all feels like yesterday, you know? The late-night café hopping, all our endless conversations...and our first kiss under that winter streetlight."

I smile, realizing how quickly she brings me back to those moments. "I love you, Prakriti," I say softly.

And right then, as if the universe is listening, our waiter shows up, perfectly timed, with our usual: coffee for me, and a plate of Prakriti's all-time favorite—momos. (I swear, momos are her true love; I'm just lucky to be in second place.) We settle back, and I can't help but keep talking about that first day we met.

"Prakriti, right over there—you were so engrossed in that book," I say, nudging the plate closer to her.

She laughs, maybe a little embarrassed, but I continue anyway. "I looked over and thought, 'There she is. My crush.' Now look at us—forever bound, as inseparable as...well, Hardy and his snacks." She's blushing, her cheeks going that perfect shade of red, and I feel like I might actually be pulling off the romantic line.

Then, like magic, she smiles, her eyes sparkling as she reaches for her coffee. I notice a tiny bit of sauce on her lip, the kind of sauce that will forever go down in "I remember that moment" history. I grab a napkin and wipe it away gently, and her cheeks turn an even brighter red.

Right, back to breaking the fourth wall for a second. Let's be honest, folks: this is what rom-coms are made of, and I'm fully aware that I'm currently starring in my own. Only, there's no background music or slow-motion shots—just me, a few laughs, and the love of my life, wondering why I keep wiping sauce off her lips like some kind of restaurant ninja.

So there we were, back in that café, talking about all the moments that brought us here, to a place I didn't even imagine back then. And for just a second, time feels like it's stopped.

So, we stepped out of the restaurant, hand in hand, and headed toward my pride and joy. Ah, yes—the *Batmobile*. And no, it's not an actual Batmobile (unfortunately). It's my black Continental GT 650—my non-sponsored, ever-loyal ride. I call it the Batmobile because, well... it's black, it's beautiful, and it's seen us through plenty of adventures. Reference alert: *Beneath the Sunset and Stars*—where it all began. (I may or may not be trying to nudge you into checking out that prequel, just saying.)

I helped Prakriti onto the bike, and we were off, cruising into the night. Her arms wrapped around me, her head resting on my shoulder—I could feel her warm breath even through the chill. It was one of those rare, perfect moments where I remembered just how lucky I am. This bike? It's been through it all with us—the good, the bad, the hilarious. Not to mention, I'm convinced it secretly plays romantic background music, but only for us.

But before I get too sentimental, let's not forget the real star of this story—Hardy, my pet turtle and the true MVP. Yes, folks, give it up for Hardy! If you're wondering why this little guy deserves a standing ovation, allow me to explain. Hardy has this incredible ability to ignore the drama in my life, focusing only on his two favorite things: food and splashing water as if he's trying to flood the apartment.

In fact, Hardy says "Hi" (or he's demanding more food—honestly, it's hard to tell with him). This turtle's got the appetite of a teenage athlete, with a hunger that could rival a black hole. If you're scratching your head wondering why I call him the MVP, let's just say he's been the surprise hero of more than a few scenes in *Beneath the Sunset and Stars*. Yes, yes, I'll stop the shameless promotion, but seriously—Hardy earned his title fair and square.

But back to this moment. The night air whipped past us as we rode, Prakriti's laughter soft in my ear every time I took a slightly faster turn than necessary. I could feel her smile against my back. The streetlights blurred into long stretches of golden light, and the city around us started to quiet down, leaving just us, the open road, and the steady hum of the engine.

Then, as we slowed down at a red light, Prakriti leaned in close and whispered, "Thank you, Gaurav. For everything."

I wanted to say something smooth, something memorable—but all I managed was, "You know, I'm the lucky one here." A bit cliché? Maybe. But I meant every word.

We continued riding, weaving through the city streets, until we reached our favorite spot—the riverbank overlooking the Brahmaputra. We parked the bike, and she climbed off, taking my hand as we walked to the edge. The moonlight danced across the water, and everything was still. No words, just us.

"Do you ever think about what it would've been like if we'd never met?" she asked softly, almost as if talking to herself.

I squeezed her hand. "Can't imagine it," I replied. "Honestly, I think fate—and maybe a little bit of Hardy's stubbornness—would've brought us together one way or another."

She laughed, shaking her head. "So Hardy's responsible for our love story?"

"Of course," I said, smirking. "He's the mastermind. He's probably at home right now, plotting our entire future together, with a side plan for extra food."

We both laughed, and I realized once again how much joy she brought into my life. We stood there, hand in hand, watching the river. This was one of those moments that didn't need anything extra—no grand gestures, no elaborate speeches, just her, me, and the quiet night.

But, of course, knowing Hardy, he'd want me to wrap this up so we could get home and give him his well-deserved second dinner. So, yes, folks, that's where we were—at the riverbank, staring out at the world together, wondering where life would take us next... and maybe, just maybe, planning the quickest way home to keep the MVP happy.

Note from the Writer *: "Welcome back, dear readers! If you've made it this far, it means you're just as invested in Gaurav's life as he is in that Continental GT 650 of his—and yes, that's saying something. I'd like to believe this chapter is where Gaurav's journey takes a tender, almost cinematic pause. We've got romance, humor, and even a turtle with an appetite that could rival a small black hole.*

If you're here wondering why Hardy gets such a spotlight, well, I'll just say this: every rom-com needs a wildcard, and what's better than a turtle whose main priorities are food and chaos? Gaurav might think he's the hero of his own story, but let's be honest, Hardy's the real MVP here.

Anyway, while I'm here making Gaurav wax poetic about love and "what ifs" by the riverbank, I'll admit—I'm fully aware of how he'd rather not let me make him sound so sentimental. But hey, that's what I'm here for. So settle in, keep turning those pages, and enjoy every laugh, awkward pause, and tender moment. After all, life's all about those small, unforgettable memories that Gaurav's doing his best to navigate...with a little help from Prakriti, and of course, our favorite turtle sidekick.

Until next time—enjoy the ride!"

2

When Your Dinner Guests Are From the Other Side

❤

So, here we are, in a new rental house. Fresh walls, bigger rooms, a fancy study I can pretend to work in—all the upgrades. At first, everything seemed perfect. A little too perfect. Then I noticed something strange: the room was *colder* than outside. Now, sure, that sounds like a perk—no more sky-high AC bills, right? (That's my idea of optimism, folks.) But jokes aside, it wasn't just cool. It was cold. *Bone-chillingly* cold.

And to top it off, Prakriti wasn't around. She'd gone home for a few days to do the "Let's Convince Mom About My Love Life" tour. How's that going, you ask? No idea. Probably better than my new situation here. But anyway, that left me all alone. Well, *almost* alone. Hardy was here too, keeping it real with his usual demands: food, water splashes, and zero concern for the strange vibes lurking in our new place.

I decided to keep it a surprise from Prakriti—a bigger space, a study room, a whole lot of mysterious charm, and a vibe that practically whispered *plot twist*. Romantic, right? Except, after a few days, the excitement was slipping into something else. Something... weird. You know that feeling you get when someone's watching you? Except you turn around, and there's *no one there*. Yeah. That kept happening. And every time, the feeling grew stronger, like a pair of eyes just moving out of view but *never leaving*.

But maybe it was all in my head, right? I told myself that as I took a puff of my cigarette, feeling the silence settle around me. Just me and Hardy here, and Hardy, of course, didn't care. He was just chilling in his tank, munching like there was nothing odd about a house that feels like the set of a horror movie.

And let me tell you about this place: it's got this massive layout. Starts with a huge hall, a small room on the left, a basin (strangely placed) near two bedrooms, then a big kitchen, another bedroom, a balcony at the end, and a lone bathroom that looks like it belongs in a haunted film. At night? It's eerie. Shadows lurking, corners I didn't remember being that dark. I tried convincing myself it was just my overworked, sleep-deprived brain talking. But the vibe was off. *Way off.*

Fast forward three days in, and things started getting stranger. Sometimes I'd find half-eaten food in the kitchen, usually my carefully cooked chicken (hey, I need protein). Now, my first guess? A stray cat sneaking in through an open window. But every window was locked. Every door secure. So, what was it? Paranormal food theft? I didn't have an answer, but I tried to ignore it. Hardy? Completely unfazed. He was on some zen-level peace, munching away while I was slowly questioning reality.

One night, while doing my usual Netflix-and-chill routine (no sponsorship, by the way, but Netflix, feel free to reach out), I heard a soft cry echoing from the balcony. I paused. *Nah, probably just a stray animal.* I went back to my show, ignoring the slight shiver crawling up my spine. Then it happened again. This time, louder. I muted the series, ears tuned to the silence, but the cry stopped. My brain, ever the skeptic, chalked it up to sleep deprivation and moved on.

But then, an hour later, I heard it again—clear, almost mournful, like someone was right outside. I grabbed my phone (also not sponsored by Apple), flipped on the flashlight, and started down the dark hall. And yes, I know—no lights installed yet. Just a bulb in the kitchen and one in my bedroom. The rest of the place? Practically a cave. Call it laziness, call it denial, but I'd been living in semi-darkness for days. I could already hear Prakriti's voice in my head: "Oh come on, Gaurav, you're not Batman!" If only.

So, flashlight in hand, I made my way through the shadowy halls, each step accompanied by that creeping feeling of being watched. I reached the balcony door, took a breath, and opened it. Nothing. Just the night air, thick and cold. I laughed it off, but then—*CRASH!* Something hit the kitchen floor. My chicken. *Again.*

"Okay, so what now? Ghosts have a taste for rotisserie?" I muttered, bracing myself as I checked every corner of the kitchen. Nothing. The food lay there, half-eaten, but no sign of a stray or a ghostly dinner guest.

And if you think Hardy cares? Not at all. Our MVP is back there, chilling in his tank, probably doing imaginary high-fives while I question reality. "Real nice, Hardy," I mutter, as if he's in on some joke.

The days went on, and the strange incidents piled up. Sometimes, when I'd be working, I'd catch movement from the corner of my eye—something or *someone* darting by, disappearing just as I turned. Every night, the crying sound grew louder, closer, like it was moving through the walls, inching toward me.

Then, one night, I was in bed with the door closed, watching Netflix, when I heard a faint tap on my door. A pause. Then another tap, like something—or someone—was testing the lock. I sat up, pulse racing. I'd had enough of the creeping dread. I grabbed my baseball bat, swung open the bedroom door, and stepped out, bat in hand, ready to channel my inner action hero. "Alright, buddy, whether you're a ghost or a thief, let's settle this. IT guy or not, I'm about to take you down," I said, wielding the bat like I knew what I was doing.

I took a slow, steady breath, scanning the dark corners. Then I felt it. Someone was behind me. I swung around, bat raised, but the hallway was empty, only the dim glow of my phone lighting the way. My instinct screamed, *balcony*. Every horror movie trope told me not to go, but my other side—the side that does all-nighters and debug marathons—said, *Bring it on*.

So, there I went. Hardy, still in his tank, barely looked up. "A little support would be nice," I muttered, eyeing him as if he'd help. But he just blinked, chewing on his lettuce like, *You got this, boss*. Real encouraging.

The balcony was dark, just shadows and silence. I took a cautious step forward. Then another. And then, suddenly, the air felt heavy, pressing in on me. I turned, heart racing, and caught a glimpse—a flicker of something, a shadow moving *fast*. I held my breath, gripping the bat harder, ready to swing.

And then—nothing. Just an empty hall, the darkness somehow thicker, heavier.

I shook my head, muttering to myself. "Alright, I've had it. If you're a ghost, thief, whatever, I'm right here. And for the record? I've got a black belt in judo. So, you wanna fight? Let's go!"

I heard a snicker. Low, echoing. I whipped around. Standing at the far end of the hall was a shadow—a figure with hair cascading over her face, eyes gleaming, a twisted grin. Her laugh echoed through the space, bouncing off the walls. Every horror film cliché and survival instinct kicked in, but my pride wasn't about to back down.

"Alright, you think this is funny? Guess what—I've got the ultimate move ready," I said, trying to sound as confident as possible. "Yeah, I know it's illegal, but this is life or... whatever you call your afterlife. Yagura Nage. Look it up."

I took a deep breath, channeling all my judo practice. I moved forward, one step at a time, until I was within reach. Hardy, from his tank, looked like he was cheering me on. *Go, sensei, go!*

The figure lunged. Instinct took over—I reached out, grabbed her by the arm, and executed the throw, feeling her weight shift as I put all my strength into it. She hit the ground, hard, then disappeared in a swirl of black smoke.

Panting, I dropped the bat, a grin spreading across my face. "That's right. Don't mess with a guy who pulls all-nighters on caffeine and debugging."

Hardy, meanwhile, was doing a little celebratory dance in his tank, probably imitating the Ninja Turtles. Or maybe he was just happy to get back to his snacks in peace.

I stumbled back to bed, heart pounding, but victorious. But as I lay down, my vision blurred, and the walls seemed to close in around me. My eyelids grew heavy, and I drifted off, feeling a strange chill settle over me.

Just as I slipped into sleep, I heard it again—a soft laugh, echoing through the dark.

Note from the writer: *Ah, the perks of a new place—bigger rooms, fresh walls, and, apparently, a ghost with a taste for midnight snacks. Following Gaurav's journey from Netflix binges to ghostly home runs has been a wild ride, and if there's one thing I've learned, it's that even the bravest IT guy can be rattled by a well-timed creak in the dark. And, of course, Hardy the turtle remains as unfazed as ever, our reliable MVP.*

So, grab your bat, your flashlight, and maybe an extra piece of chicken—because this story is only getting stranger. Stay tuned, because in this haunted rom-com, the unexpected is always right around the corner!

3

Of Spirits, Sleep-Deprivation, and Summit Surprises

---◦♡◦---

My visions were still blurred out, the only thing on my mind being how I'd see Prakriti again. The fear of the spirit? Gone, poof! I suddenly jolted awake, and there she was, Prakriti beside my bed, looking all concerned.

"Is everything okay?" she asked, her eyes wide, scanning my sweaty body like I was a new case study in her journal.

"I saw the strangest dream," I replied, still trying to shake off the remnants of my nightmarish escapade. Seriously, it felt so real. Like, "I almost had a spirit smackdown" real.

"You should stop watching those haunted documentaries," she teased, arching an eyebrow.

"Hey, it's not like that!" I protested, inching closer and planting a soft kiss on her forehead. "It was an epic battle!"

She smiled back, a mix of concern and amusement. "Okay, let me brew you some coffee."

As I swung my legs over the edge of the bed, I thought, "Remember chapter 16, 'Tears and Triumphs'? This is why I'm banned from the kitchen."

I shuffled to the kitchen, still a bit dazed. Coffee? Check. Bacon? Check. And let's be honest, who doesn't love a side of crispy fat to start the day? The aroma was heavenly, and my stomach growled louder than Hardy when he's ready for a snack.

Lost in thoughts about the bizarre dream, I reached for the hot pan, and—ouch!—I burned my finger. No yelp, no dramatic flailing, because I knew I was one more incident away from a lifetime ban in the kitchen. And trust me, the last thing I needed was another episode of "Gaurav the Kitchen Disaster."

"Hardy, say good morning to all the readers," I said, turning to my turtle, who was basking in the light like he owned the place. I swear he has an uncanny ability to gauge my mood. Maybe he's plotting his own spin-off series.

I tossed him some pellets, and he looked thrilled, probably thinking, "Ah, the same food again! What a gourmet meal."

With two steaming cups of coffee and a plate of bacon, I tiptoed back to the bedroom. "Breakfast is ready!" I declared, planting a kiss on her lips, hoping my culinary skills wouldn't come into question.

She put her laptop aside, a smile lighting up her face. "I really love the way you pamper me. I'm getting spoiled, you know?"

"I love doing this for you," I said, slipping a piece of bacon into her mouth like I was some kind of breakfast waiter. "And don't worry; I'm totally fine with being the sous-chef for a while."

"Just don't set the kitchen on fire again, okay?" she teased, taking a bite and eyeing me like I was a potential arsonist.

"I promise nothing!" I replied with a grin, knowing full well I could accidentally ignite my culinary ambitions.

As the daily grind began, there I was, the IT guy in his chair, fingers dancing over the keyboard like I was some kind of tech wizard. Meanwhile, Hardy gave me a look that said, "Shameless human, remember who the real boss is here."

"Listen, Hardy," I said, looking at him pointedly, "you may have a cool shell, but I'm the one who feeds you, okay? You're lucky I'm not putting you to work. Who knows? Maybe you'd be better at debugging than I am."

And there we were, three characters in a comedy of errors—me, Prakriti, and Hardy—living life one laugh, one ghost encounter, and one plate of bacon at a time. So, dear readers, stick around! In this story, the absurd is just the warm-up act, and trust me, the real show is just beginning

Note from the Writer:*Hey, wonderful readers!As you dive into Gaurav's world, I hope you find joy in the mix of humor and the supernatural. This chapter highlights the sweetness in his relationship with Prakriti, balancing kitchen disasters with heartfelt moments.*

Thank you for joining me on this quirky journey. Your support inspires every word, and I can't wait to share more adventures with you!

So here we were, Friday night in all its glory, the night we'd both been counting down to. And, yes, as any seasoned couch-surfing, tired-of-the-9-to-5 warriors know, Friday night means *extra* booze. I'd planned a proper unwind session for Prakriti and myself after a week that felt like a brutal wrestling match with code. Some misguided soul once told me, "IT jobs are a breeze," and let me tell you, I'm now actively hunting for that person.

With the stage set for a "Netflix and definitely not sponsored" night, it was just the three of us: Prakriti, Hardy, and yours truly. Of course, my genius self decided to ignore Prakriti's morning warning of "No haunting documentaries tonight," because, well, apparently, I'm *that guy* who thinks "just one episode" won't hurt. Prakriti, on the other hand, was the epitome of multitasking—wine in one hand, her laptop perched on her lap as she tinkered with her journal, and her eyes glued to the screen like she was solving a murder mystery herself. Occasionally, she'd take a moment to greet Hardy, who seemed content as ever, his beady eyes darting between us and his turtle-sized Jacuzzi.

It was a particularly tense scene in the documentary, the type that makes you clutch your blanket a little tighter, when suddenly—*ding dong!* The doorbell rang. We both nearly leaped out of our skins, and Hardy, well, he blinked once. *Maximum turtle reaction, right there.*

I got up, muttering to myself, "If this is the spirit from my dream come for a rematch, I swear, I'm ready." Taking a deep breath, I swung open the door, and standing there was none other than Prakriti's cousin, Niku—the same guy I'd, um, accidentally judo-slammed in *Beneath the Sunset and Stars*. Yes, that's right! Spoiler alert for the readers who haven't picked up my book yet (which you totally should, by the way, because indie writers need love too). But I digress.

"Surprise!" Niku grinned, extending his hand. I shook it, trying to mask the faint embarrassment of our last encounter. "Hey! Good to see you. Come in!"

"Oh, so something's going on here," he teased as he stepped inside, giving Prakriti a knowing look.

"Oh, we absolutely knew you'd be dropping by at 2 a.m., so we prepared this entire 'Netflix and Wine' presentation just for you," Prakriti quipped, rolling her eyes.

Niku laughed, taking a seat and accepting the glass of whiskey I offered. "So, what's up? Watching haunted documentaries again, huh?" he smirked, clearly amused at my self-inflicted terror. "Don't tell me you're planning to judo-slam every ghost in your dreams now."

"Look, let me set the record straight—last night's spirit didn't stand a chance!" I declared. "But let's not dwell on my heroic exploits."

"Sure, sure," he chuckled, settling back into his chair, "So, I actually came over to see if you guys would be up for a trek tomorrow."

"A trek?" I raised an eyebrow, intrigued. "Where to? And with whom?"

"Oh, just us three," he replied, then turned to Hardy with a grin. "Sorry, Hardy, no turtle-sized trekking boots yet."

Hardy, in classic turtle fashion, looked completely unimpressed. It's like he was saying, "Excuse me, do I *look* like I need boots? I've got a Jacuzzi."

"That's a surprise!" Prakriti said, finally looking up from her laptop. "Though Gaurav here had plans to, well, 'get wasted' tonight. Isn't that right?" She shot me a mock glare over her glasses.

"Okay, alright, 'getting wasted' is officially canceled," I admitted, putting my hands up. "Trek plan, it is! Besides, Hardy, I swear, we're taking you surfing one day."

Hardy blinked, clearly indifferent. His world revolved around pellets, water, and the occasional sunbath.

"So, guys, it's already 2 a.m.," Prakriti said, glancing at her phone. "Are we planning to go on this trek sleep-deprived, or are we chugging caffeine until sunrise?"

"Just a quick power nap," Niku suggested confidently, as if he was a motivational speaker on a TED Talk stage. "We'll leave at 4 a.m., get to the spot by 5 a.m., and the trek starts bright and early."

"Oh, no problem," I said, serving up the last of the dinner Prakriti had magically whipped up while we were watching. Seriously, she's like the ultimate multitasker. "Hey, how about we just stay up and load ourselves with caffeine? Who's in?"

"Or," Prakriti said, adjusting her glasses and sipping from her wine, "we take a nap and save ourselves from complete zombie mode tomorrow."

As we cleared up, the lights went off one by one, our little apartment winding down to recharge just enough for the crazy idea we'd signed up for. Hardy was already cozied up in his corner, probably dreaming of sunlit rocks, while we slipped into a two-hour "power nap" that felt suspiciously like fifteen minutes.

I have to admit, as the three of us (well, minus Hardy) embarked on our spontaneous trek at the crack of dawn, I felt a strange rush of excitement. Maybe it was the sleep deprivation. Or the caffeine. Or just the promise of doing something insane, with people who made every moment memorable. Either way, here we were—ready for yet another wild chapter.

Note from the writer:_Hey there! Thanks for tagging along with Gaurav, Prakriti, Hardy, and, well... all the random chaos. Writing these moments—whether it's late-night laughs, haunting dreams, or impulsive trek plans at 2 a.m.—feels like letting you in on the inside jokes. If you're here, you're part of the crew, navigating all the quirks, mishaps, and "brilliant" plans with us._

And yeah, for every indie writer, it's tough to get our stories out there, so every bit of support you throw our way is like gold. If you laughed, cringed, or rolled your eyes reading this, that's the dream.

So, buckle up! There's more madness coming.

The alarm on all three of our phones went off like a bomb—an unholy trinity of sounds that shook the night. We looked like zombies; I mean, imagine us, all bleary-eyed and still slightly buzzed. Why did we think a 4 a.m. trek on zero prep and maybe two hours of sleep was a good idea? And yet, somehow, there we were, trudging toward the trailhead in the misty cold. Hardy, our turtle, was probably having the best time at home, all cozy and snoozing while we stumbled around like amateur adventurers.

"So... here we are," I muttered as we started climbing. "Fresh mountain air, sleep-deprived, and totally prepared."

"Totally prepared," Prakriti said with a dry laugh, grabbing her energy gel. She looked half-awake, but still had that determination you only see on people who don't realize what they've signed up for. Niku gave her a thumbs up, which meant absolutely nothing.

Ten minutes in, and our bodies were already screaming at us. It felt like the trek itself was judging our life choices.

"How much further?" I gasped.

"It's been like ten minutes," Niku replied, wheezing. "Just... keep going."

Prakriti, trying to pep us up, added, "The view is going to be amazing, trust me! I saw it on Google."

Right. Because if it's on Google, it must be worth it. That didn't stop us from hiking up, though. I downed some water, practically inhaling it like a camel, and kept trudging.

Then, out of nowhere, I spotted... something. A long, thin, black leg hanging from a tree. It looked creepy—way too creepy. I froze.

"Hey, uh, guys?" I whispered, staring at the mysterious limb.

"What now?" Prakriti grumbled.

I pointed. "Look. Over there. Is that... a leg?"

"Oh my god," she said, squinting in horror.

"Maybe it's a spirit, coming for a rematch from my nightmare!" I blurted out.

"Okay, Gaurav, be serious," Prakriti said, shooting me a look that was part annoyance, part "You're ridiculous." But deep down, I was actually serious. I mean, sleep-deprivation plus hangover hallucinations? Very possible.

We crept closer, bracing ourselves for battle. And guess what? It was a branch. Yep. A branch. We had almost fought a tree, folks. In my head, Hardy was probably facepalming, if turtles could.

"Bravo, brave warrior," Niku snickered. "First tree you see, you're ready to judo slam it."

"Hey, I was prepared, okay?" I defended myself. "You never know with these misty woods. They practically scream Wrong Turn vibes."

We laughed it off and kept going, fueled by the adrenaline of almost getting attacked by a... tree. After an hour, though, we reached the peak. And, honestly, it was worth every miserable, caffeinated, sleep-deprived second. We were above the clouds, with this endless view stretching out in front of us. Instagram, eat your heart out.

Of course, after a mini photo session and wolfing down snacks, it was time to head back. That's when Niku decided to take us down a "shortcut."

"This'll save us so much time," he said confidently.

Spoiler alert: it didn't. We got lost. Because, of course, in the middle of a dense forest, everything looks the same. And to make matters worse, Prakriti tripped, hurting her ankle pretty badly.

"Ow! I can't walk," she said, wincing.

My heart dropped. "Are you okay?" I asked, kneeling down to check her ankle. Thank god I'd packed a first-aid kit, but still, it looked rough.

"You okay, DiDi?" Niku asked, looking guilt-ridden.

"It's not your fault, Niku," Prakriti said, tough as always, but I could tell she was in pain.

"Don't worry," I said, trying to sound way cooler than I felt. "I'll carry you." I gave her a little forehead kiss, and even though she was hurting, I could see a small smile. So, I tied her to my back with a scarf like some DIY piggyback setup and started down the trail.

Now picture this: me, a human backpack, hauling her down a mountain. And in the middle of all this, we come across a family of monkeys chilling out. Cute, but also a little intimidating—just like, don't get in my way, I'm trying to save my damsel here.

"Look at these guys," Niku whispered, cracking a smile. "They're just watching us suffer."

"Yeah, just wait 'til one of them asks us for directions," I muttered, doing my best to ignore my aching shoulders.

After what felt like forever, we heard cars honking in the distance. Civilization! We practically ran toward the sound, delirious with relief. I swear, the sight of that road was more beautiful than the trek view itself.

A quick stop at the hospital later, the doctor told us Prakriti's ankle was just a sprain—she'd be fine in a few days. Huge sigh of relief. In the car ride home, Niku was driving, while I sat in the back with Prakriti, holding her hand.

But as we stopped at a traffic light, I glanced out the window... and my stomach flipped. There, across the street, was a building that looked exactly like the haunted house from my dream. And I could swear—could swear—I saw a face peeking out from one of the windows, grinning that same eerie grin.

The light turned green, and the car pulled forward. I sat there, cold with goosebumps, wondering if we'd just barely escaped a rematch after all.

Note from the Writer: *Hey, fellow night owls and adventure lovers! Thanks for sticking with Gaurav, Prakriti, and Niku on this sleepless, hangover-fueled trek. If this chapter reminded you of one of those times when a "great" plan turns into an absurd adventure, then mission accomplished. It was a blast to add a few extra layers of chaos to their day and sprinkle in some laughs (and a bit of terror—because who doesn't love a good ghost scare?).*

If you're wondering if that spooky house will make a comeback... well, let's just say that once a spirit catches your scent, it's hard to shake them off. So keep your eyes peeled and lights on! Until next time—keep trekking, even if the path is as lost as this one turned out to be.

4
The Turtle Seal of Approval

The déjà vu hit hard. I watched Prakriti leave, déjà vu-ing like a pro—same clothes, same smile, even the same "bye" in that lilting, singsong tone. And Hardy? My turtle wasn't missing a beat, splashing around with his usual zest. Honestly, the guy does this all the time, so maybe he's the one in a loop, not me. But here I was, alone in the house for the first time in ages. It's for a good cause, I reminded myself. Prakriti was off to try and convince her mom about *us*, and as much as I missed her already, it felt like a fair trade.

"Okay, focus, Gaurav," I muttered to myself, booting up my laptop. "I have work to do." But of course, it was only thirty minutes into her absence before I caught myself zoning out. Was I really this much of a romantic sap? Fine, yes. Guilty as charged. Back to reality! I had a whole IT project to tackle, after all. Yet, as I stared at the screen, my mind drifted back to *her*. Or, rather, to *it*—the spirit from my recent dream.

What if... she was real? Waiting for a rematch, maybe? The memory of that unearthly wail made my skin prickle. Okay, okay, snap out of it, Gaurav. No ghost would be haunting me while I'm debugging code, right?

Switching mental gears, I reminded myself that it was my turn to talk to *my* parents about Prakriti. Part of me had expected some Herculean task ahead, but, surprise surprise! The moment I mentioned Prakriti's name, my dad lit up. "How did *you* manage to get a girl out of your league?" he asked, laughing. I just gave him a confident smile (that, let's be honest, was maybe a 4 out of 10 on the confidence scale).

"We're happy for you," he added, surprising me even more. "Bring Prakriti over sometime to meet us."

"Sure! She'd love to," I replied, feeling relieved. Mom chimed in next. "Let's be real here, Gaurav. You put in zero effort in winning her heart. It's all Hardy's doing, isn't it?" She smirked knowingly.

And Hardy? Oh, he was just basking in the limelight. I could practically hear him laughing: *This guy can't do a thing without me.*

"Hey, hey, I had some hand in it too," I protested, stumbling over my words.

Mom looked me straight in the eyes. "Is she happy with you?" she asked, her tone softening.

"Yes," I replied with a wide grin. "It feels like I'm on top of the world with her."

"And are you happy with her?" she asked again, the ultimate mom follow-up.

"Yes, absolutely," I said, feeling the warmth of the words.

"And the most important question: Did Hardy approve of this relationship?"

"Mom, Hardy is more thrilled than I am! I think he loves Prakriti more than me, to be honest," I admitted, side-eyeing Hardy, who was practically glowing with smugness.

"Then you have our blessing," she said, with a contented smile. Well, there you have it, readers—Hardy is officially the MVP. Maybe I should've titled this book *Hardy: The Real Hero*?

One hurdle cleared, but the next one loomed: Prakriti's family. She's an only child, and I wasn't sure how they'd take the news. And of course, Hardy, that little show-off, kept telepathically telling me, "Relax, Gaurav. My charm could melt the Himalayas." Sure, Hardy, sure.

Three days passed. Just three days! But it felt like three years. I missed Prakriti like crazy, and Hardy seemed to be feeling it too. The two of them had this weird telepathic connection going on, and he seemed to be sulking without her around to feed him. I tried to keep things normal, texting Prakriti late into the night, just like old times. We laughed, reminisced about our café-hopping days, and she teased me for being so nervous to confess my feelings back then. It's hard to believe we've been together for over five years now. Five years! Time really does fly when you're an anxious mess in love.

Then, out of the blue, Prakriti texted: "I told Mom about us. She invited you over for lunch the day after tomorrow."

Lunch. With her mother. In two days.

Oh, and it's on a Monday, my busiest workday! How on earth was I going to explain this to my manager? But I'd do it, whatever it took. After all, Hardy has somehow won over everyone in my life—manager included. Never underestimate the power of a turtle with charisma.

The night before The Lunch, I made a plan. I put together a suave, black outfit, smelling faintly (or maybe overwhelmingly) of my best cologne. I have a minor... obsession with cologne. One for every occasion. I rehearsed my lines, mentally playing out every scenario, every question. Hardy, the little mastermind, was just watching me with an amused look, as if saying, *Bro, relax. Drop my name, and her mom will love you. You're practically invincible with Hardy in your corner.*

Then—classic me—I did something spectacularly clumsy. Browsing through Instagram, I somehow found myself on Prakriti's mom's profile, and... I accidentally liked a very, very old photo of hers. Smooth, right? I panicked, unliking it immediately, but the damage was done. I had officially doomed myself.

"What's wrong with you, Gaurav?" Hardy's telepathic voice groaned. "First, you like her daughter's ancient photos. Now her mom's? She's going to think you're stalking the family!"

I spent the rest of the night in damage-control mode, barely able to look Hardy in the eye. *Why do you keep doing this to yourself, Gaurav?* My mind ran in circles.

Note from the Writer:*Ah, here we are again, my dear readers—trudging alongside Gaurav on his path of delightful blunders and epic turtle-induced rescues. If you think navigating a relationship is tough, try doing it with Hardy, the MVP turtle, in the mix. Gaurav's life might look like a hot mess of Instagram slip-ups and déjà vu-driven panic, but let's be honest, who isn't rooting for this guy?And if you're wondering about the countless references to Hardy's charms—believe me, they're warranted. This turtle might just be the glue holding Gaurav's life together. So, as you flip these pages, remember that love isn't always grand gestures and romantic speeches. Sometimes it's the humor in the stumbles, the midnight rehearsals, and, yes, the accidental likes on very old photos.*

Sit back, laugh, and maybe relate a little too much as Gaurav fumbles through love, family approvals, and the occasional ghostly worry. After all, life's a bit of a comedy when you think about it—especially with Hardy calling the shots.

So here we are. After an absurd number of rehearsals, a mountain of overthinking, and several... *unfortunate* Instagram likes, the day has arrived. Today's mission: Prakriti's house, for the Grand Meet-the-Family event. And no, I won't be on my bike. Today calls for something special. Introducing my most prized possession: the black BMW 2 Series Gran Coupe 220d M Sport. Yep, if this were flexing, I'd be Arnold in a car showroom.

(Oh, and spoilers, readers—this car isn't just for show. It's got a future role that's worth the ride.)

Now, let's address the obvious. I'm a bike person. But today, this car feels right. Prakriti's house is about 100 km away, so I've got enough time to cycle through my mental checklist of potential screw-ups. Upon reaching, I sent a casual "Love, I've reached." Prakriti's response? "Don't screw this up." Classic Prakriti—straight to the point.

And then she stepped outside. No words. I mean, *literally no words.* She looked like an absolute vision.

"Wow," I said, almost forgetting the flowers in my hand.

She sized me up with a smirk. "You look like you're auditioning for Batman," she teased, glancing at my all-black ensemble.

"Well, Gotham needs me," I replied, handing her the bouquet. I even threw in some sweets for extra points. "You think I'll pass the test?"

"Obviously," she laughed. "You're my guy, aren't you?"

Feeling the jitters? Me? Never! Okay, maybe a little. But onward, soldier. We marched toward her house, which I expected would involve a quick meet with Prakriti's mom. Just her mom, right?

Plot twist.

27

I stepped inside, and *bam*—her uncle, aunt, a scattering of cousins, and her grandmother. The room was practically a mini family reunion. At this point, even my mental checklist was like, "Bro, you're on your own."

I plastered on my best smile. "Namaste, aunty," I greeted Prakriti's mom, praying the sweat didn't show through my shirt.

"Please, have a seat, Gaurav," she smiled back. And so, I stepped into the *hot seat*, ladies and gentlemen. Prakriti's cousins were eyeing me like I was the final boss in a game they were ready to tackle. I took a deep breath, channeling my inner Hardy. Yes, the turtle. Because, as we all know by now, Hardy's my ultimate backup.

I spotted Prakriti's grandmother and quickly walked over to touch her feet. "Namaste, dadi. I'm Gaurav," I said, hoping my voice didn't betray my nerves.

"Oh, *you're* Gaurav?" she said, a smile lighting up her face as she patted my head. "Prakriti tells us all about you."

Prakriti, looking all innocent, gave me a little shrug as if to say, "Yeah, I bragged about you. Deal with it."

We settled in for what I knew was about to become the Q&A round of my life. The cousins sat around like a jury, her mom with her "I can see through your soul" smile, and Prakriti's dad with a quiet, observing look that had me questioning all my life choices.

"So, Gaurav," her dad began, "tell us a bit about yourself."

"Oh, well, I'm in IT," I began. "Mostly coding, some project management..."

Ding!—first invisible point goes to me for getting through that question without fumbling. Next question: her uncle leaned forward with an eyebrow raise.

"And you're okay with Prakriti's... er, independent nature?" he asked, obviously fishing.

I glanced at Prakriti, who was now staring at me like she was daring me to fumble.

"Oh, absolutely," I said, trying to keep it cool. "Actually, her independence is one of the things I admire most about her. It's like having my own, personal superhero."

Her cousins giggled, and Prakriti's mom seemed pleased. So far, so good.

Then, dadi leaned in with the kicker. "So... Prakriti says you have a turtle?"

And there it was. Hardy, the turtle, was making his grand entrance into the conversation. I could almost hear him snickering in my mind, like, *See, I told you. Just mention my name.*

"Yes, dadi! His name's Hardy. He's practically family." I grinned, suddenly confident.

Dadi laughed. "A turtle named Hardy. That's a new one. But I hear he's very... *helpful.*"

"Oh, incredibly. He's my little good-luck charm," I said, giving Prakriti a wink.

From there, the questions got easier—thank you, Hardy! I started to feel like I was back in the driver's seat, steering the conversation and actually enjoying myself.

Just then, Prakriti's dad leaned over. "So, Gaurav, when do you think you're ready to... you know, settle down?"

And just like that, my heart did a backflip. This was it—the ultimate question.

I glanced at Prakriti, who gave me an encouraging nod. "Honestly, I think I've been ready since I met Prakriti," I said, looking straight at her dad.

He nodded, then gave a small smile. "Then you have our blessing, Gaurav."

Cue the mental victory dance. Internally, I was doing cartwheels. I almost wished I'd brought Hardy just so he could witness my triumph in person.

As we wrapped up, Prakriti's mom leaned in with a smile. "One last question, Gaurav... did Hardy approve of Prakriti?"

I looked over at Prakriti and then said, "He definitely did. Actually, I think he likes her more than he likes me."

With that, the family laughed, and I knew I'd passed the test. We'd survived the day with only minor bruises to my ego and one near-miss with an out-of-syllabus question.

As we left, Prakriti gave me a soft smile. "See? Told you not to screw it up."

I grinned. "Yeah, yeah. But just wait till I bring Hardy next time. Then you'll see real charm in action."

Note from the Writer: *Welcome back, dear readers, to yet another chapter of Gaurav's ever-epic love life! Who knew navigating romance would require the skills of a seasoned detective, the nerve of a spy, and, apparently, the charm of a turtle? Yes, Hardy, the turtle, is the unsung MVP, and Gaurav wouldn't have survived this Q&A gauntlet without him.*

This chapter was a ride in itself. What started as a simple meeting-the-family plan turned into a full-blown exam of nerves and wit for our protagonist. After all, how many of us can handle "out-of-syllabus" questions from all the extended relatives?On another note, this was the first time Gaurav and Prakriti's family world really intersected in a way that tests both humor and heart—a blend I hope you enjoyed as much as I did writing it. We're gearing up for more twists, and let's be real: with Hardy as our spirit animal, the journey is bound to be entertaining.

Thank you for being here, for rooting for Gaurav (and Hardy, of course), and for laughing along with each chaotic, heartfelt moment. Stay tuned, because if you think the family meet-up was intense, just wait till you see what happens next.

5

The Dr. Cancer Chronicles

———————◦♡◦———————

The aftermath of the grand family interrogation left me feeling like I'd crossed a marathon finish line. The good news? Prakriti was finally back! Those days without her had felt like some drawn-out survival test. Sure, Hardy, my ever-loyal turtle, was there, but he's more of a passive listener. Prakriti, on the other hand? She's like my oxygen. Yeah, I know, that sounds like something right out of a sappy romance novel, but hey, it's true.

She was barely through the door before I blurted, "Do you have any idea how much I missed you?"

She smirked, putting down her bag. "You're telling me? I thought I'd have to get Hardy to babysit you just to keep you sane!"

"Oh, he tried," I said, giving Hardy a proud nod. "The guy's my wingman, therapist, and apparently the secret to winning over your family."

She laughed, moving closer. "I'm proud of you, though. Not a single embarrassing blunder?"

"Well, one of your uncle did ask if I was okay with your... 'independent nature.' And I think your grandmother might think Hardy is some sort of... super turtle."

Prakriti chuckled. "Maybe he is. Now you can't complain about my superhero obsession if Hardy's basically the Samuria of turtles."

Then she dropped the big news.

"Oh, by the way, I got the job!"

"What?! You mean—"

"Yes!" she grinned. "Assistant Professor. Gauhati University. Starting next month."

"Professor in the house!" I shouted, giving her an exaggerated bow. "Ladies and gentlemen, Dr. Prakriti has entered the chat!"

She laughed. "Thank you, thank you. It's funny, though. I thought this PhD would be the last thing, you know? Now everyone's asking about a postdoc."

"Postdoc?!" I gasped, clutching my chest in mock horror. "Are they going to make you Assistant Professor Extraordinaire now?"

"Apparently, there's no end to the studying. One step at a time, though."

I gave her a look. "Are you sure they're not just making things up to keep you around? Like 'Doctor' wasn't enough?"

"Oh, stop it," she said, giving me a light shove. "Besides, you're one to talk. You practically live at your computer, tinkering with code like it's an ancient language you need to decipher."

"Touche," I admitted. "Though, between you and me,"—I turned toward the readers—"she might actually be addicted to degrees. I'll let you in on a secret: Prakriti's an unstoppable study machine."

She looked at me, raising an eyebrow. "Are you... monologuing again?"

"Oh, you know me," I said, shrugging. "Gotta keep the audience updated. It's like a public service."

She rolled her eyes, fighting back a smile. "Well, keep monologuing. I'm off to get changed. And don't mess with Hardy's ego too much while I'm gone."

As she left, I looked over at Hardy, who seemed to smirk as much as a turtle can. "Looks like we did it, buddy. I'm officially dating Dr. Assistant Professor Prakriti, future Postdoc Wonder Woman, with a fan club consisting of... well, mainly you and me."

And Hardy? He gave an approving splash, practically oozing smugness. The little guy's loving this, trust me.

Note from the Writer: *Ah, dear readers, where do we begin? Our protagonist, Gaurav, has just survived what can only be described as a rite of passage: the grand family interrogation. It's no easy feat winning over one's future in-laws, but with a little help from his ever-stoic turtle, Hardy, he's managed to pull it off (albeit with a few amusing misunderstandings along the way).*

And now, the news we've all been waiting for—Prakriti has returned! The ever-curious academic has added another impressive line to her resume as an Assistant Professor at Gauhati University. Gaurav, of course, reacts with all the enthusiasm of a man who believes he's dating a superhero (which, let's be honest, he sort of is). And as if that weren't enough, Prakriti's sights are set on something even more daunting: a postdoc. Yes, the journey from "Dr. Prakriti" to "Professor" seems never-ending.

Meanwhile, Gaurav continues to play the loveable narrator, breaking the fourth wall as naturally as breathing, giving us a peek into his thoughts about the woman who's become, as he puts it, his "oxygen." With Hardy's silent but smug approval, he's accepted his role as Prakriti's biggest cheerleader—and our unofficial storyteller.

So here's to Gaurav, Prakriti, Hardy, and you, dear readers. The journey is just beginning, and, if Gaurav's ramblings are any indication, it's bound to be a delightful mix of awkward charm, fourth-wall-breaking humor, and a whole lot of heart.

A few months had passed, and while Prakriti was now wrapped up in her new teaching role, my days weren't exactly dull. I had Hardy's silent-but-judgmental company as I debugged code late into the night, which sounds great—until you realize Hardy isn't much for small talk. Still, there was one unexpected new twist in my life: I had a rival. Not a coding rival, mind you, but someone worse—a *romantic* rival.

Enter "Cancer." Yeah, that's what I've decided to call him, partly because of his zodiac sign but mostly because he's a walking irritation that just... spreads. This guy is like a rom-com cliché with no off switch, constantly hovering around Prakriti, trying to "help" her in ways that only scream "notice me."

And the worst part? He's got this weird "too-caring" vibe, as if he doesn't realize she's already committed—or maybe he does, and that's the point. Ugh.

One afternoon, I tried to play it cool. Prakriti and I were texting, and she casually mentioned Cancer had made some "joking" comment about her favorite movies in class.

"Wow, he's... persistent," I said, typing carefully so my phone wouldn't pick up on the anger radiating from my thumbs.

She laughed, sending a emoji. "Oh, he's harmless. Just being friendly."

"Friendly? He's practically moonwalking into the 'Please Notice Me' Hall of Fame," I replied, half-joking but also 100% serious.

"Hmm," she typed back. "Someone sounds a bit... jealous?"

"Who, me? Jealous?" I replied, feigning innocence, but inside, I was practically combusting. I decided to switch tactics. "By the way, you know he's probably the type who thinks 'sarcasm' is a brand of cologne."

"Oh, stop," she wrote, probably rolling her eyes. "Besides, he's actually quite smart."

"Smart? He's as mature as a teenager at a rock concert. I make a single sarcastic comment and he pouts like I've insulted his whole family tree. And don't get me started on how he likes and comments on all your pictures before I even see them."

"Oh, come on," she laughed. "He's just quick with his notifications."

"Yeah, quick to annoy me," I muttered. "It's like he's allergic to me but won't stop buzzing around."

The next day, Cancer was back at it, and, as usual, with no subtlety whatsoever. Prakriti and I were meeting for coffee after her class, and, lo and behold, Cancer "just happened" to walk by.

"Oh, hey, Prakriti!" he said, giving her a big, beaming smile. "Nice to see you here. Out for coffee? That's great! You deserve a break after that lecture."

I sat there, trying my best not to roll my eyes so hard they'd fall out of my skull. "Yeah, she definitely deserves a break... *with her boyfriend*," I said pointedly, looking at him.

He paused, his smile slipping ever so slightly, but he recovered with a shrug. "Hey, I get it. Don't worry—I'm just a colleague."

"Right. And I'm just an unpaid Hardy apprentice," I replied, glancing at Prakriti, who was holding back a smirk. "Anyway, have a nice day, Cancer."

As he walked away, I leaned closer to Prakriti. "I swear, if I could just judo-slam him once—*just once*—I'd sleep better at night."

She giggled, patting my hand. "So much fire, Gaurav. I thought you were all Zen and peace."

"Oh, I am," I replied, grinning. "It's just that Cancer's like this recurring background irritation. Like, at this point, I'm convinced he's here to test my moral values."

And then, as if he somehow knew I was talking about him, Cancer turned around and gave Prakriti a little wave. I gritted my teeth, turning to the readers.

"See what I mean?" I said, raising my eyebrows. "I'm like a walking fire hazard with this guy around, and he has the audacity to be offended when I clap back."

Prakriti nudged me, laughing softly. "Oh, don't worry. I'm sure Hardy would help hide the evidence if you ever did decide to judo-slam him."

"Maybe," I mused, a mischievous glint in my eye. "But there are ethics and moral values, right?"

And Hardy? Well, he just gave me his usual, knowing look.

After weeks of enduring Dr. Cancer's never-ending antics, my patience had worn thin. This guy was on my nerves, like an alarm clock that never stops going off. Every morning, he'd send Prakriti a cheerful "Good morning!" message, and every night, a "Good night!" Like, doesn't he have anything better to do?

I tossed and turned each night, wondering how long I'd have to deal with this walking irritant. Just once, just *one* excuse, and I'd judo-slam this guy so fast he'd question his life choices. And that's when I started to silently beg our dear author for a setup—a chance to teach this guy a lesson.

And wouldn't you know it? The author obliged.

One fine morning, after a sleepless night, Dr. Cancer strutted up to me with a smug grin. "Hey, I heard you know some judo?" he asked, leaning in, his tone dripping with condescension.

"Yeah, a bit," I said, trying to keep it casual, even though my blood was practically boiling.

He laughed. "Let me guess, a few YouTube tutorials?"

I forced a smile. "Something like that," I replied, my mind already racing with a series of throws I could try on him.

He kept going. "I actually took some judo back in college. Got myself a nice yellow belt." He puffed his chest, looking around for any impressed stares.

A yellow belt. Really? *Oh, buddy,* I thought. *You've got no idea.*

But I kept my poker face. Prakriti, meanwhile, gave me a look that said, *I know where this is going.*

Dr. Cancer finally bit. "So, how about a friendly match? I'd love to see if all those YouTube tutorials actually taught you something."

I nearly laughed out loud. This guy had no idea he was challenging a fourth-degree black belt. "A match?" I said, feigning uncertainty. "Sure, why not? But maybe somewhere private?"

The Head of Department, overhearing this exchange, looked amused. "No harm in a friendly match in the office, right?" he said with a shrug, giving us the green light.

And there it was. Game on.

In minutes, we'd rearranged the office, transforming it into an impromptu judo dojo. A crowd gathered, with everyone trying to act like they were working, but really, they were just waiting for a show. And I wasn't about to disappoint.

37

As we squared off, I could feel Prakriti's eyes on me. Her look was clear: *Go for it, Gaurav—but don't actually break his bones.*

Cancer took his stance, clearly underestimating the wall of throws he was about to meet. And before he could even process what was happening—bam! A quick throw sent him flying onto the mat. He got up, slightly dazed, but still not catching on. Another throw—bam!—and then another, until finally, I wrapped it up with a classic Sode Tsurikomi Goshi.

For those of you wondering, that's a shoulder throw that practically sends your opponent into orbit. Feel free to Google it.

Cancer lay there on the mat, his brain and his pride both bruised. It was all he could do to muster a breathless, "I quit."

I reached out to help him up, trying my best not to smirk too much. "Oh, by the way," I said, "I forgot to mention I'm a Black Belt, Dan 4. That comes before yellow, right?"

There were a few chuckles, a smattering of applause. The HOD himself chimed in, "Prakriti, looks like you've got a loaded bazooka on your hands!"

Everyone was clapping now, and I couldn't help but notice the glances exchanged around the room. Turns out, I wasn't the only one who found this guy annoying.

Dr. Cancer, meanwhile, was still trying to process the utter beatdown he'd just received, and for a moment, I almost felt bad. Almost. But then I remembered all those "Good morning" and "Good night" messages, and my sympathy evaporated.

Thank you, dear author, for this glorious setup. It's not every day a character gets to take their frustration out on an actual person, much less in front of an approving audience.

And so, dear readers, that's the end of Cancer's chapter—a hard lesson learned.

Note from the Writer:*Ah, here we are, folks! It's been quite a journey, hasn't it? Gaurav has just faced off with his romantic rival in what can only be described as a masterclass in "carefully planned" office drama. When you're caught in the crossfire of someone like Dr. Cancer—a determined suitor oblivious to personal boundaries—it's only a matter of time before things escalate.*

But, really, who knew that a judo match would be on the agenda? It's not every day you get to see an everyday coder take down an over-eager romantic rival with fourth-degree expertise, all in front of an enthusiastic office crowd. Gaurav's subtle jabs at the readers along the way have kept us thoroughly entertained, and Hardy, ever the silent judge, is no doubt cheering him on in his own, turtle-y way.

So here's to Gaurav, to Prakriti's effortless charm, to Hardy's silent but steady support, and to you, dear readers, for witnessing "The Dr. Cancer Chronicles." Remember, every love story has its trials, and, in Gaurav's case, sometimes those trials just happen to involve a bit of judo.

6
The Chaos Chronicles of Princess the Destroyer

Time, that curious friend we barely notice as it dances by, pulling us along its winding path. It feels like just yesterday Prakriti and I were strangers in a café, caught in that delicate dance of first glances, unaware of what was yet to come. I remember our late-night rides through the city, every café venture that felt like its own small adventure, and that unforgettable bike ride to Kaziranga. Ah, dear readers, if you remember *Beneath the Sunset & Stars*, you remember the confessions and the winter streetlight that, somehow, gave me the courage to say those words to her.

As I swam in the nostalgia of these memories, lost in thought, there was a sudden, sharp knock on my door. The kind of knock that yanks you back to reality. It was Sunday—a day I'd designated as "Victory Day" for successfully surviving my showdown with Dr. Cancer. Just a beer for celebration, you know? And, in a twist, Hardy was all over the floor today, exploring every corner. I'd seen an Instagram reel where someone placed a tiny skateboard under their turtle's belly, and, suddenly, I knew what my next mission would be. But, before I could go DIY with Hardy's potential new ride, another knock sounded.

"Who could it be?" I muttered to Hardy, who, as usual, offered no insight.

When I opened the door, there they were: Koushik, Priyanka, and the legendary Destroyer—a name that makes the dog sound like a fierce, battle-hardened beast, when in reality, Destroyer is a Chihuahua with the spirit of a dinosaur and the size of a potato. Oh, and yes, I may have given him the name "Destroyer," but Koushik went with "Princess." Yes, Princess. For a male Chihuahua. Who knew irony could be so tiny and so yappy?

"Hello," I said, looking down at Destroyer, who, as usual, was eyeing Hardy's tank with intense curiosity.

"What brings you guys here on a Sunday?" I asked.

"Well, I'm here because I heard my character development was getting limited airtime. Had to change that," Koushik replied with a smirk.

"But this is my story," I replied, resisting the urge to remind him who's supposed to be the star.

"I know, but the writer gave me a hint," he said, nudging me and breaking the fourth wall with more ease than he breaks a bag of chips. "Maybe my story arc is just getting started."

"Well, good luck with that, my friend," I laughed, rolling my eyes.

"Stop breaking the fourth wall, Koushik," I sighed, ushering him and Priyanka inside. No sooner were they in than Koushik spotted my beer on the table, casually popped the cap off, and took a long sip.

"Where are your manners, Koushik?" Priyanka scolded, giving him a look that could tame a lion—or at least a Chihuahua.

"Hey, Prakriti!" Koushik greeted as she came out of the kitchen, waving warmly. Meanwhile, Priyanka unleashed Destroyer—aka Princess—who bolted straight to Prakriti. It's like he has some sixth sense about her; he's all over her every time he sees her. I swear, Prakriti has this strange talent of speaking animal language, like a Dr. Dolittle for the miniature breed.

"Look at him go," Prakriti said, laughing as Destroyer pranced around the room. Meanwhile, Hardy—the silent observer—seemed unimpressed. You could practically see the rivalry heating up between these two: one a battle-hardened turtle, the other an excitable Chihuahua. Stay tuned for their ongoing saga.

After we all settled, Koushik cleared his throat. "So, actually, we're heading on a little trip, and we were wondering if you guys could watch Princess for a few days."

"Destroyer, with us?" I echoed, weighing the pros and cons of having him around. It's not that I have anything against dogs—quite the opposite—but Destroyer has his... quirks. Trust issues, to be specific. With everyone. Especially Hardy.

"Oh, I'd keep her forever!" Prakriti exclaimed, looking way too thrilled as she reached down to pet Destroyer. "I mean, he's adorable, and I've missed having a dog around."

"That settles our worries, then," Priyanka said, looking visibly relieved.

"So, where are you two headed?" Prakriti asked, pouring tea for everyone.

"We're planning to explore Meghalaya," Koushik replied. "Outskirts, waterfalls, the whole nature package."

"Oh, you'll love it," Prakriti said, her eyes lighting up. "It's beautiful there—perfect for some downtime."

And so, we spent the next hour chatting, mostly about Destroyer's dietary quirks and Meghalaya's scenic trails. Before long, Koushik and Priyanka left. And, dear readers, mark my words: Koushik, Priyanka, and the relentless Destroyer will return in the future. After all, the writer has big plans for them—and for me, if I survive this Chihuahua's reign of chaos.

Now, dear readers, if you're scratching your heads wondering who Koushik is, let me remind you—this is the same guy from the prologue of *Beneath the Sunset & Stars*. If you're here without having read the prequel, you're getting spoilers, my friends. It's not a promotion, just a heartfelt suggestion: *Beneath the Sunset & Stars* is where it all began. Go give it a read, and then come back—I'll wait.

Alright, back to the story. Destroyer—yes, Princess the Destroyer—is now at my place, and as usual, Prakriti's giving him all the love in the world. And it's funny because, even though Destroyer (let's stick with that) loves Koushik, he seems pretty attached to me, too. He'll jump up, lick my face like it's the best part of his day, and trot around my legs with an energy level I didn't know Chihuahuas could achieve. But don't let the cuteness fool you; this dog is pure chaos.

Let's get into phase one of Destroyer's antics. I'm going about my day when I hear an odd sound coming from the kitchen. There's Destroyer, proudly gnawing on the gas cylinder pipe. Not the pipe, Destroyer, anything but the pipe! I rush over and pull him off, only for him to dart across the room, my poor purse in his mouth. In seconds, he's shredded every important document I had. ID cards, insurance papers—everything. And as if that weren't enough, Destroyer once blessed Koushik's laptop screen with his... personal brand of eau de Chihuahua.

"You little monster," I mutter as he darts away, tail wagging. Meanwhile, Hardy is watching this spectacle from his tank, completely unamused. You'd think he's silently judging this dog, the audacious visitor who dared to invade his territory.

Prakriti, of course, finds all this endlessly amusing. "You know, he's really just misunderstood. I think he's charming."

"Charming? This dog bit through the gas pipe! We're lucky the house didn't blow up!" I say, exasperated.

"Maybe he's just full of energy. You know, like a Red Bull," she laughs.

"Red Bull? I swear, this dog is the devil's own Red Bull. They should make him the new mascot. 'Red Bull gives you wings—and a new reason to hide your valuables.'"

She laughs even harder, while Destroyer's busy eyeing my laptop like it's next on his list. I make a mental note to hide all electronics before he strikes again.

Monday arrives, and I'm working, deep into debugging some code. Prakriti's out at her job, and it's just me, Hardy, and Destroyer. I'm in the zone, completely absorbed, until something doesn't feel right. It's too quiet.

"Princess?" I call, glancing around. No answer, not that I expect one. I look over at Hardy, who's staring at me like, *Don't look at me, he's your problem now.*

Suddenly, I realize Destroyer is nowhere in sight. Panic mode, activate.

"Oh no," I mutter, throwing on my shoes and rushing out the door. "Destroyer! Destroyer, where are you?"

I search every corner of the colony, calling his name (and getting some seriously strange looks from neighbors). I'm about to lose hope, imagining the worst—that he's run off to terrorize a highway or bark at some poor passing car—when I finally spot him.

And there he is, the little devil, strutting around the center of a massive dog gang like he's their leader. Six local street dogs stand around him in a circle, all looking suspiciously submissive. And then, for the cherry on top, there's a massive cow in the background, looking oddly wary of Destroyer, like even it knows this tiny creature means trouble.

"Oh my god," I whisper, taking in the scene. Destroyer has them all under his spell. I half-expect him to start barking orders.

I approach, and one of the bigger dogs looks at me with relief, like, *Thank you, human, for taking this demon away.*

"Destroyer," I say firmly, scooping him up. "You are grounded for life."

Destroyer wags his tail, completely unrepentant. Behind me, the six dogs and the cow let out collective sighs of relief as we walk away.

When we get back, I set Destroyer down in the living room, hands on my hips. "Do you have any idea how much you've aged me today? That stunt with the dogs and the cow was... impressive, but dangerous!"

Destroyer just tilts his head, his big brown eyes full of mischief.

Prakriti walks in, eyes wide. "Did he actually lead the local dog gang?" she asks, stifling a laugh.

"Oh, he didn't just lead them. They were terrified of him! And I'm pretty sure the cow is sending thank-you vibes as we speak."

"Well, guess you've got a mini-supervillain in the house." She grins. "Just think—one day, you'll look back on this and laugh."

"One day? I'm still recovering from the gas pipe incident, and now I have to worry about him staging a coup with the local wildlife."

I glance over at Hardy, who's still watching with that trademark turtle judgment. "See, Hardy agrees. Destroyer's out of control."

And just as I say this, Destroyer trots up and gives my ankle a playful lick, wagging his tail. Maybe he's not so bad after all.

So, dear readers, if you're reading this and think Destroyer sounds like a handful, let me tell you—you're right. But that's what makes him one of a kind. And, Red Bull, if you're reading this, the Destroyer is ready for his brand deal. Terms and conditions apply.

Note from the writer: *Dear readers, welcome to yet another chapter of untamed antics and ridiculous rivalries. Here we have Princess the Destroyer, a Chihuahua with the soul of a rebel leader, stirring up mischief and becoming the bane (or perhaps secret joy) of Gaurav's life. Whether it's rallying the local dog gang or befriending a cow, Destroyer seems determined to add a bit of unexpected excitement to every moment. And yes, Red Bull, if you're still considering it, Destroyer's energy could sell itself—no marketing needed.*

7
The Great Biryani Battle

It was just one of those days, you know? I ordered biryani on a whim, because really, who needs an excuse for biryani, right? I had the plate in my hands, ready to savor each spicy, fragrant bite, when Prakriti walked in from work. Now, dear readers, you might assume couples fight over big issues—trust, commitment, time management. Nope. *We* fought over a plate of biryani.

"Did you order biryani without me?" she asked, eyeing the plate.

"Uh...maybe?" I replied, trying to act casual, but let's be honest, biryani is never casual.

Her eyes narrowed. "And you didn't think to order an extra one?"

"Prakriti, it was a last-minute decision!" I stammered, clutching my biryani like it was the last on earth. "I thought you'd already eaten!"

"Are you kidding me?" she replied, inching closer, hands on her hips.

"Look, I can get you a spoon?" I offered, lifting my spoon defensively.

She snorted, but took the spoon. And thus began the Great Biryani Battle. We didn't speak for a solid hour afterward. Silence, dear readers. Just the quiet tension of a plate of biryani sitting between two people.

Later that night, after a few hours of cold shoulders and side-eyes, I took a deep breath and made a "sacrifice." "Fine, you can have the biryani," I said, pushing it toward her.

"Oh, I'm fine," she replied, crossing her arms. "I didn't really want it."

Inside, I was rejoicing. More biryani for me! But I kept up the act, playing it cool. "Oh, great. I don't want it either."

We sat in silent, stubborn standoff, both staring at the biryani as if it were a ticking bomb. But I couldn't take it any longer. Finally, I reached for a bite. Just one bite to hold me over, I told myself.

Of course, that's when she spoke up. "Actually...maybe I'll have some."

Caught mid-bite, I mumbled, "Of course, sure. I'll just feed you a spoonful."

And there it was—our makeshift truce. I'd give her one spoon, then take two for myself, stealthily, trying to out-eat her.

Hardy, watching from his tank, looked horrified, as if to say, *Not the biryani again. You two are ridiculous.*

And in the corner, Destroyer lay sprawled out, completely oblivious, giving me that little side-eye that said, *Humans, am I right?*

Just when I thought we were finally reaching a balance, Prakriti snatched the plate away. "You know what? I'll just finish it. You had most of it anyway!"

"Oh no, you don't!" I countered, grabbing the plate back. At this point, it was more about principle than actual hunger. We were two full-grown adults—one a senior

48

software developer, the other an assistant professor with a doctorate—locked in a full-scale biryani battle, as if the fate of the universe depended on it.

And so it went, spoonful by spoonful, until there wasn't a single grain of rice left.

As we finished the last bite, we both looked at each other and burst out laughing. "Why does biryani always bring out the worst in us?" I asked, shaking my head.

"I have no idea," she replied, smiling. "But maybe next time, we'll just order two plates."

But knowing us, dear readers, we'd probably fight over whose plate looked bigger. Ah, the things we do for love—and biryani.

Note from the writer: *Hello, fellow biryani lovers and laughter enthusiasts! Sometimes it's the smallest things that spark the most memorable battles. Here, we witness Gaurav and Prakriti in a classic standoff—proof that, in the world of love, no plate of biryani is safe. It's a reminder that even the little quarrels hold their own charm, creating memories worth savoring. And, let's be honest, when biryani is involved, it's never "just food." Cheers to all the quirky moments that make relationships feel uniquely ours.*

8
The Uncharted Road

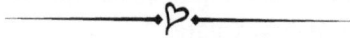

It was early morning, just a hint of dawn peeking through our bedroom window. The smell of chocolate lingered in the air—my secret "mountain" of chocolates and a hidden cake all waiting on the dining table. I leaned over and hugged Prakriti, whispering, "Happy anniversary, love." She woke up, a smile breaking across her face, and planted a kiss on my lips. Sometimes, I still can't believe how fast time flies when you're with the right person.

"I want to stop time when I'm with you," I said, gazing into her eyes.

"I feel the same, Gaurav," she whispered, her hand resting on my cheek.

"Alright, up we go!" I said, lifting her into a piggyback ride toward the dining room, where candles flickered around the cake. Her eyes shone with surprise and... was that a tear?

She hugged me tightly and our lips met again. "Thank you for making every moment so special," she said, her voice soft.

We cut the cake together, and even Hardy joined the celebration from his tank, splashing around as if he understood the occasion. Prakriti dropped a few pellets in for him, and he looked as happy as a turtle could.

Then, leaning in close, I whispered, "And guess what? We're going on a road trip to Meghalaya today."

Her eyes widened in excitement. "Are you serious? I'm so ready!" she exclaimed, practically jumping in place.

"Not on the bike this time," I grinned, "we're taking the car."

Her brows lifted, and she laughed. "You're telling me, *you*—Gaurav, the 'I-live-for-the-thrill' bike guy—chose the car?" She smirked, amused. "Who are you, and what have you done with my boyfriend?"

"Call it a hunch, love," I replied, shrugging. "Something tells me it's a 'take the car' kind of trip."

We packed up, both dressed in black to match the sleek look of my BMW 2 Series Gran Coupe 220d M Sport—an all-black beauty that felt right for the adventure ahead. "Hardy's all set too," I assured her, setting up his automatic feeder and light.

The drive itself was enchanting, with mist hanging over the mountains like a veil, and the road winding around us in beautiful curves. Prakriti was snapping photos of everything for her Instagram dump, determined to make her friends envious. When we reached Laitlum Canyon, she was positively ecstatic.

"You know, most of the time, this place is a foggy mystery," I told her. "But with you here, the view is clear. See? You're my lucky charm."

That got me a playful punch in the arm and a smile. We even camped out with locals that night, sharing stories by a warm fire.

The next day, we hit up Dawki, where the water was so clear you could practically see the fish winking at you from under the boat.

Finally, we spent a night in Shillong, where I surprised Prakriti with a lucky bamboo plant for her university desk. "Look at you, so thoughtful," she teased. "And here I was thinking you were only thoughtful about biryani portions."

"Well, Hardy doesn't settle for anything less than imported gear, so he's all set too," I joked, which got me an eye roll and a smile.

After a couple of days of exploring, it was time to head home. Everything was smooth on the highway, the car purring along, until a group of bikers appeared out of nowhere. They were weaving through the road, cutting in and out with that reckless thrill of invincibility. One moment, they were laughing and swerving, and the next—a bike skidded, a scream, and in the blink of an eye, my instincts took over.

I swerved, trying to avoid the tumbling rider. Time slowed as the car veered off course, and the world tilted. I heard Prakriti's gasp, my hands clutching the wheel as we rolled off the road.

The next thing I knew, silence.

My eyes fluttered open, and everything was upside down. My head felt like a fogged-out dream, throbbing, and I struggled to make sense of the scene. "Prakriti?" I called out, reaching over. She was slumped against the seat, a trickle of blood on her forehead. "Prakriti!" I shouted again, desperation seeping into my voice.

I could hear my heartbeat hammering in my ears as I reached for her hand, squeezing it, pleading for any sign. "Come on, Prakriti... wake up, love. Say something. Please." But all I got in return was silence.

This wasn't how our trip was supposed to end. This wasn't part of the "Happy Anniversary" plan.

Just as I felt my own consciousness slipping, I whispered one last promise: "Hang in there, love. I'm not letting go..."

Note from the writer:*The best-laid plans can go awry, dear readers, especially when "driving instinct" tells you to take the car. From magical anniversary moments to harrowing twists, sometimes life has its own plot twists that no amount of planning can anticipate. So here's hoping for safe journeys and safe returns—and remember to trust your gut... and maybe, just maybe, avoid the crazy bikers.*

9
The Abyss and the Warrior

As consciousness returned to me, I blinked open my eyes in a sterile white hospital room, the beeping of machines around me feeling more like a slow, echoing drumbeat of dread. My head throbbed as if I'd been hit with a steel bat, but none of that mattered—I had to find Prakriti.

"Prakriti!" I tried calling, but my voice cracked, hoarse, like I'd been screaming for hours. I struggled out of bed, barely able to stand straight, the hallway tilting with every step. *Where is she? Why isn't she here?* Every face around me blurred, like looking through a misted window, but my feet dragged me forward, down the hall.

And then, at the end of the corridor, there she was. Prakriti, lying in a hospital bed. My parents, her family, even cousins I'd never seen before, stood around her. A silent, sorrowful circle, with tissues crumpled in their hands and red eyes staring down. I staggered toward her bed, my pulse racing.

"Doc," I croaked, barely able to get the word out. "Doc... please, tell me... Prakriti's okay, right?"

The doctor's gaze dropped, his hand resting lightly on my shoulder, but that weight felt like it carried the world. "I'm so sorry. She sustained a severe head injury... we couldn't save her."

No. No, this isn't real. I tried to reach her, shaking her gently. "Prakriti... come on, love. You promised you wouldn't leave me, remember?" But she lay there, cold and unresponsive, as if even my words couldn't reach her anymore.

A month later, life had become a dark, hollow version of itself. Hardy, my little turtle, barely moved, his tiny face pressed against the side of his tank as if he too were searching for her. I hardly ate, barely slept. Each night, I would close my eyes and wish not to wake up the next day, but Hardy... well, he was always there, staring with those round eyes, as if he was all that was keeping me here.

Months had gone by, yet the pain was just as raw. I'd become a recluse. Every call ignored, every friend turned away. I took to walking in the park just before dawn, seeking some kind of peace in the mist and silence. It was there I first saw her.

She stood at the edge of the fog, long black hair trailing down to her hips, her pale face almost luminous against the grayness. She wore a black gown that clung to her form, and her eyes were like dark wells that drew me in.

I blinked, sure it was a trick of my exhausted mind. But the next morning, she was there again. And the morning after. Each time, she was in the same place, with the same strange smile.

On the fourth day, as I walked past her, she reached out and grabbed my hand. Her grip was ice-cold, and her gaze... it felt like it was piercing straight through me. She started muttering strange words, a chant that grew louder, echoing around us like a loop. Before I could pull away, the world around me started to spin.

Suddenly, everything went dark, then snapped back into focus. We were no longer in the park. I was standing before a towering, dark mansion, its walls twisted with vines, the windows hollow and black, as if they were hungry eyes watching us.

I knew this place. It was the house from my nightmares—the one that had haunted me ever since the accident.

"Welcome to my humble abode," she sneered, her voice dripping with malice as she drifted toward the doorway.

"Who are you? What do you want from me?" I shouted, but my voice barely echoed in the silence.

"Oh, poor Gaurav, so in love," she cooed, mocking me. "Don't you understand? I had to take her from you to weaken you. You were far too strong with her by your side."

"You took her from me?" I felt anger flare up inside me, making my hands shake. "Why? What did we ever do to you?"

She laughed, the sound like nails on a chalkboard. "Oh, it wasn't my choice, Gaurav. I'm merely a servant, summoned by someone... someone you know well."

My heart dropped. *Someone I know?* My mind raced through names, but none of it made sense.

"So, Prakriti..." I choked out, feeling tears prick at my eyes. "She's really gone because of... you?"

"Oh, Gaurav." She raised her eyebrows, mocking me with a smirk. "Not because of me. Because of someone you trust."

Suddenly, I heard it—a voice, faint but unmistakable. *Prakriti's voice.*

"Gaurav... don't believe her!"

56

"Prakriti?" I shouted, my voice breaking. "Where are you? Prakriti!"

The spirit laughed, her form flickering like a dying flame. "Oh, she's here, alright. But there's no way you'll reach her. You're stuck here, with me, until you break. Until you give up all hope."

Her words struck me like a blade, slicing through the last of my strength. I fell to my knees, despair weighing me down, her laughter ringing in my ears.

Then, a deep voice boomed from behind me. "Enough."

I looked up, eyes wide. A tall, muscular figure stepped forward, dual katanas glinting in his hands. He was dressed in gleaming black armor, and his eyes were fierce and unwavering.

"Master," he said with a slight bow. *Wait... Master?*

"Hardy?" I stammered, barely able to believe my eyes. My turtle, my little Hardy, was standing before me in the form of a warrior, his calm, unblinking eyes filled with fire.

"Indeed, Master. I am here to protect you," he replied with a calm nod, as if his transformation was the most natural thing in the world.

"Hardy! You—uh, where did you get the katanas?"

"I have always been prepared, Master," he said with a small smile, before turning to the spirit. "Now, let us settle this."

In a flash, Hardy launched himself at the spirit, his katanas cutting through the air with incredible speed. She shrieked, her form scattering into fragments, but each fragment regenerated, multiplying into more spirits that crowded the dark hallway.

"You think you can defeat me?" she cackled. "You are nothing without Prakriti!"

Hardy's gaze sharpened, his resolve unbroken. "Master," he called to me over the noise, "you must hold onto hope. Your strength comes from within, from your love, not from her games."

At that, something within me snapped back into place. I rose to my feet, feeling a warmth flood through me. Hardy was right. I couldn't let this twisted spirit play with my mind.

In one final surge, Hardy chanted an incantation, his katanas glowing bright. He slashed through the spirits, each one dissolving until the room was finally silent.

"Master," he said, sheathing his katanas and extending a hand to me. "It is time to go."

"But... Prakriti—"

"Trust me, Master. She awaits you."

With that, Hardy took my hand, and once again, everything blurred.

Note from the writer:*Hey there, dear reader! So, let's talk about what you just read. You're probably wondering: why did Hardy, the peaceful little turtle, suddenly turn into a katana-wielding, spirit-slicing samurai? Great question! It was either that or a rock-paper-scissors showdown with a supernatural entity (and trust me, I considered it).*

In storytelling, sometimes it's about balancing moments of intense grief with a dash of the unexpected, a pinch of humor. That's where Hardy comes in, embodying the fierce protector we didn't see coming, but perhaps Gaurav needed all along. And honestly, wouldn't we all love a pet that would fight off literal ghosts for us?

Writing this chapter, I wanted to explore Gaurav's journey through grief, loss, and a hint of the supernatural mystery that somehow all makes sense within this strange, labyrinthine narrative. Hardy's transformation might seem surreal, but hey, sometimes life's most meaningful moments are. And remember: just when things feel their darkest, help might arrive from the most unexpected places.

10

Back from the Edge

———❦———

As my vision slowly cleared, I found myself back in a bright, familiar hospital room. A swarm of blurry shapes hovered around me, but one came into focus—Prakriti. She was holding my hand so tightly that I could feel the tremor in her grip. Her face was streaked with tears, eyes swollen, but despite that, she'd never looked so beautiful.

"Pra...kri...ti..." I croaked, barely recognizing my own voice. I could feel my throat scratch like I'd been screaming all night. "Is it...really you?"

"Yes, Gaurav! It's me!" she sobbed, squeezing my hand harder, almost like she was afraid I'd disappear if she let go. "I thought I'd lost you... Oh my god, I was so afraid!" Her words tumbled out in a mix of relief and laughter, and she wrapped her arms around me, burying her face in my shoulder.

"Whoa, okay, don't break any ribs now," I murmured, groggy but thrilled, as I awkwardly patted her back. "I'm a little too handsome to be squished to death."

She laughed, despite her tears, and wiped her face, still clutching me tightly. "I'll squish you as much as I want!" she replied defiantly, her voice full of that familiar

60

stubbornness. "Do you have any idea what you put me through? Three days, Gaurav! You were in a coma for three days!"

"Three days?" I tried sitting up, and my head spun, making the hospital room spin like a carousel. "Wait, wait, back up. Coma? Three days? I... I thought... we were..." Images from that nightmare flickered in my mind, flashes of a wrecked car, the mansion, the haunting figure. And Hardy... with katanas? Oh no, did I actually hallucinate my pet turtle as a ninja warrior?

"Yes, three days," she repeated, dabbing at her eyes, then grinning through her tears. "And you're... you're okay. Just a bump on the head. You're the same silly Gaurav I know. No extra brain damage."

"Well, that's reassuring." I gave her a weak thumbs-up, doing my best to ignore the confused looks from my friends and family around the room. "But seriously... what actually happened? Last thing I remember was swerving the car and then... everything went black. Didn't we, like, roll down a hill and end up upside down or something?"

She shook her head, her brow furrowing. "Gaurav, we didn't roll down anything. You hit the railing, and we just... stopped. We were fine. The car's safety features kept us from getting even a scratch. You just... passed out from shock, I guess."

I blinked, trying to reconcile her words with my bizarrely vivid memory. "So... no mansion, no spirit lady trying to ruin my life, and Hardy wasn't actually wielding katanas?"

A few people chuckled, but Prakriti just stared at me, bewildered. "Um, Gaurav, you've had a lot of sedatives. You should probably rest. You sound... like you went on a trip to some alternate universe."

"Maybe I did," I muttered, glancing at Hardy's tank near the window. He stared back at me with his usual unblinking expression, looking far too innocent. "Or maybe this little guy saved the day," I added, giving him a nod. "Thanks, Hardy. Next time, though, maybe leave the katanas at home."

Prakriti snorted, stifling a laugh. "Oh yes, our warrior turtle. He's definitely been guarding you."

I lay back, sighing, a surge of gratitude filling my chest. I looked up at Prakriti, and I couldn't help but smile, feeling like the luckiest guy alive. "You know, I don't think I could live a single second without you," I said softly.

"Too bad you almost made me find out." She smirked, but her face softened, and she held my hand, running her thumb over my knuckles. "But I'm glad you're back. And... I think we both need to focus on being here now, not in whatever supernatural fever dreams you're having."

"Good call. I think I'm done with haunted mansions for a while," I replied, raising her hand to my lips. "But just to clarify—if I ever see another mysterious figure in black, you'll be my backup, right?"

"Oh, absolutely. As long as you promise me one thing." She grinned. "No more dramatics. We've had our fair share of lifetime's worth in the last few days."

We both laughed, and I glanced over at Hardy, our unassuming, heroic turtle. "Deal. Hardy's got my back anyway, right, buddy?"

He blinked, as if considering it. Or maybe I was imagining that too, but somehow it didn't matter.

Note from the writer:*Hey there, dear reader! So, we're finally out of the dark and twisty woods—or, more accurately, the nightmare-fueled mansions and ninja turtle hallucinations. I know Gaurav's coma journey may have been a tad extra, but* *hey, love and life both have a flair for drama, right? I wanted this chapter to balance on that edge between surreal terror and the warmth of connection, to keep you guessing and rooting for Gaurav even as his world went a little haywire.*

In my mind, this chapter serves as a reset, a much-needed grounding after all the chaos. And seeing Gaurav and Prakriti with their humor, relief, and banter? That's where the real magic happens. Because what's a little supernatural adventure without someone to hold your hand, laugh at your terrible jokes, and bring you back from the edge?

Stay tuned for what's next—we're just getting started! And yes, Hardy, the trusty turtle, will probably be making some more epic cameos.

11
The Muse Intervention

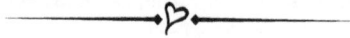

♡

The cursor blinked at me, like it was tapping its foot in annoyance, waiting for me to write the next word. Beside me, coffee cups had amassed to the point where my desk looked like a caffeine-powered pyramid—perhaps the world's most jittery architectural wonder. I took another sip, but somehow, coffee wasn't sparking any inspiration this time. Gaurav and Prakriti were frozen in my mind, caught in a scene that had replayed so many times it felt like a broken record.

Suddenly, there was a shuffle behind me. I turned, half-expecting a late-night hallucination, but there they were—Gaurav and Prakriti, arms crossed, looking distinctly unimpressed.

Gaurav was the first to speak, hands in his pockets, raising an eyebrow. "So, what's the holdup?" he asked, glancing at my screen. "We've been waiting in that café for days. I can recite the specials by heart now."

Prakriti nodded, her expression sympathetic but tinged with impatience. "I get it. Writer's block is a real thing. But... could you maybe just... imagine a bit? Or type anything?"

I groaned, slumping in my chair. "You don't think I've tried that? The ideas aren't coming. It's like my brain is stuck on standby."

"Maybe it's because you keep using us as your caffeine lab rats." Gaurav gestured toward the coffee cups. "I'm beginning to think caffeine's turned on you."

Prakriti chuckled. "You know, it's kind of ironic. You created us, but now we're the ones reminding you to keep going. Remember why you started all this?"

"Yeah..." I sighed, rubbing my forehead. "I just—look, I wanted this book to feel special. But it's hard to be 'special' when all I've got is a blinking cursor that's judging me harder than you two are right now."

Gaurav leaned over, resting his elbow on the pile of coffee cups, looking far too relaxed for a fictional character trapped in his own storyline. "I don't mean to brag, but have you tried thinking like me? Just wing it. Go off-script, toss in some chaos. If it's horrible, it's horrible. But maybe that's the fun of it."

"Chaos, huh?" I gave him a wry smile, glancing at Prakriti, who shrugged with a grin. "Fine. How about this: You two get into a hilarious argument over something ridiculous. Like... Prakriti accidentally orders chicken biryani when you wanted the mutton one."

"Oh, here we go," Prakriti rolled her eyes. "You know he'd act like the world was ending if that happened."

Gaurav feigned offense. "Excuse me! Food preferences are sacred. I think that argument could give our story some real flavor."

I laughed, finally feeling a spark of inspiration come alive. "See? Now we're talking. Maybe the biryani incident snowballs into an argument, and you both end up reminiscing about how you first met. Then it somehow segues into that trek scene I've been putting off writing for ages."

Prakriti grinned, nudging me. "See? It's all there. You just needed us to remind you why you're doing this—and to keep the

65

storyline moving, please. We're dying to see what happens next."

"You know what?" I said, rolling up my sleeves. "You're right. And for the record, I'm grateful for the nudge. I'd forgotten how much I actually enjoy this."

As I finally began typing, the words flowed like I hadn't seen them in ages. I glanced back at my two unlikely muses, but they were gone—already back in their scene, waiting for me to bring them to life again.

Writer's Note: Writing can be a strange process, with highs that feel like conquering the world and lows that feel like staring at a wall for hours. Sometimes, you need a reminder from unexpected places—even the characters themselves. Thank you, Gaurav and Prakriti, for dragging me out of the writing slump. Here's hoping the rest of the journey is a bit smoother... but hey, knowing you two, I doubt it.

12

The Biryani Chronicles

———❧———

The months rolled by with Hardy still being, well, Hardy—chilled out as ever. No sign of the warrior turtle he once claimed to be. The only battles he was fighting now were against his own reflection in the aquarium and the occasional stray feather he thought was an enemy. "Look at you, a mighty warrior," I thought, shaking my head. "Fighting your own tail... again."

And then, as usual, Prakriti came over with that extra-special petting routine for Hardy. I swear, the way she cooed at him, I almost expected her to break out in song. What they talked about during those sessions was beyond me, though. I'm sure there were some turtle politics or secretive shell-related strategies being discussed, but I couldn't understand a word of it.

"Well, buddy, let's get this show on the road," I said to Hardy, scooping him up for a quick hug before we headed out for the family picnic.

The picnic. Ah, the quintessential family gathering. I don't know about you, but picnics are like the sweet spot of every family event—plenty of food, laughter, and guaranteed chaotic moment (usually involving a battle for

67

the last piece of biryani).

I fired up the engine of my black Continental GT 650—yes, folks, that sleek machine that looks like it could be in a high-budget movie about rebellion and freedom. (Royal Enfield, if you're reading this, we can totally make a deal here. Hit me up for sponsorship, I'm ready.) I revved the engine just enough to make sure everyone knew I wasn't some weekend warrior.

Prakriti hopped on behind me, her hair flowing in the wind, and—well, let's be honest—looking absolutely stunning in her dress. Seriously, this woman could make a potato sack look like haute couture. As we zoomed off toward the picnic spot, I couldn't help but steal a glance at her.

"It was just that day we met," Prakriti said, hugging me from behind and resting her chin on my shoulder. "And now, look—our parents are with us too."

My heart swelled with affection. "And every day feels like a new beginning," I said, glancing back with a grin. "Especially when I get to see you in that dress."

She playfully swatted my back. "Focus on the road, Gaurav. You're gonna end up crashing into a tree."

But how could I not look at her? "I'm never done watching you, Prakriti."

And with that, we headed off into the open road, toward more laughter, more memories, and—inevitably—more food. And no family picnic is complete without a little bit of chaos, right?

When we arrived, the usual picnic madness was in full swing. My parents were there, Prakriti's too. It was like one big happy, chaotic bunch. Everyone was setting up the food, chatting, laughing, and—I kid you not—setting up camp in the exact same spot as last year. I swear, it was like time had frozen, and the picnic had its own gravitational pull.

But I forgot one very important thing—**the biryani.** Oh, the biryani. As we all settled in, the first thing I noticed was that there was only one large pot of it. ONE. And it was already being eyed by half the family. You'd think it was the last food on Earth.

Now, I don't know if you've ever witnessed the silent battle for a plate of biryani, but let me tell you, it's a thing. There's a sort of unspoken tension that fills the air. The moment that first scoop is made, you can feel the eyes of every family member on you. It's a game of chess, except, instead of pawns, you've got elbows.

Just as the first plate of biryani was being served, my mom turned to me and said, "Don't forget, we saved you the best part." And just as I was about to reach for my share, Prakriti's dad, bless him, swooped in with a big scoop for his plate.

I swear, for a moment, I thought we were about to have a full-fledged family turf war. But, thankfully, there was enough biryani to go around—otherwise, it was going to be an entirely different story.

"Gaurav, stop hovering around the food like a hawk," Prakriti teased as I stood there, eyeing the biryani with what could only be described as a 'hungry-but-dignified' look. "There's plenty for everyone. You're not going to have to fight me for it."

"I don't know," I said with a playful smirk, "last time, I was in the middle of a family showdown. I'm just preparing myself."

"Can you imagine?" Prakriti laughed. "You and my dad, throwing down over rice and chicken."

"Honestly? It would have been epic. You've got the drama, I've got the *moves*," I winked, and she rolled her eyes in that way that made my heart skip a beat.

As the picnic went on, I couldn't help but laugh at how ridiculous it all was—the competition over food, the constant teasing, the never-ending pile of empty cups (from all the lemonade), and the way Prakriti kept making me blush with every little comment. But, in the end, it was perfect.

Family picnics were made for moments like this—chaotic, funny, a little bit awkward, and full of love. And, of course, biryani.

Note from the writer: *And there it is, folks. The family picnic with its usual mix of love, laughter, and (you guessed it) biryani. Thanks for reading, and let's just say, the next time we go out for food, I'll make sure to reserve a separate plate just for me.*

Now, I know what you're thinking: "Is that really the end of the biryani saga?" Oh, don't worry—there's plenty more where that came from.

13

A Night Beneath the Stars and Secret

———————◦♡◦———————

So, here's the scene, folks: Hardy, our "samurai," has returned to his usual life of splashing around in the water, chomping on pellets, and giving us that smug "I-run-this-house" look. There's no hint of his warrior self, but he's still Hardy, our trusty turtle. And yes, we struck a deal with him for some extra food if he'd look after the place while Prakriti and I went on our adventure. Hardy may act nonchalant, but trust me, he's not about to let his precious pellets be endangered by our absence.

Prakriti and I had planned a night out in the wilderness—a "jungle night" inspired by our own story *Beneath the Sunset and Stars.* We wanted to live the title, so to speak. We packed up everything we'd need for a perfect grilling night under the stars, complete with wine, music, and that whole picnic-in-the-wilderness vibe.

And let me tell you, it was going to be *epic.*

We loaded up the essentials, and this time, we were taking my sleek, black BMW 2 Series Gran Coupe 220d M Sport. (Quick note to BMW, if you're reading this: open to sponsorships here! Your car may or may not have saved our lives... or was that Hardy's samurai magic?) With the essentials all set, Prakriti decided she'd be driving. After all, it was her night.

Before she hit the gas, I whipped out a bouquet of flowers filled with chocolates. Her eyes lit up, and she leaned in to plant a kiss on my lips. "You spoil me, Gaurav," she said with a laugh.

"On to the mission?" I asked, pretending to be serious as I adjusted my invisible spy gear.

"On to the mission!" she replied, her grin full of excitement.

The road to the forest was long but absolutely beautiful. I'd pre-set the music to a perfect playlist of soft, romantic songs. Our voices filled the car as we sang along, probably a little off-key, but who cares? Between her smile and my bouquet of chocolates, I could already tell it was going to be an unforgettable night.

When we arrived at the spot, the forest was aglow with the last light of the sunset. We got to work clearing a spot for the tent, setting up our little campsite, and igniting the fire. Underneath the darkening sky, with stars beginning to sparkle overhead, it felt like we'd been transported into one of those epic romantic scenes from a movie. *Except this time, it was real.*

I poured us each a glass of wine, clinking mine against hers with a grin. "Here's to adventures and the love of my life," I said, holding her gaze.

Prakriti blushed, hiding her smile behind her glass before taking a sip. "You're really outdoing yourself tonight, Mr. Romantic."

"Only the best for you, Miss Romantic," I replied, giving her a wink.

The fire crackled as I started grilling some meat and veggies. The smell filled the air, and our playlist softly played in the background. It was then that I realized it was the perfect moment to surprise her with a gift—a platinum necklace I'd noticed her admiring once but hadn't bought because of the price. I had secretly saved up for it and had been waiting for the right time.

I stepped up behind her and gently placed the necklace around her neck. She froze, her hand going to her collarbone, her mouth falling open in shock as she looked down at the delicate chain.

"Gaurav..." She turned to face me, her eyes wide with emotion. "How did you even know I wanted this? It's so... it's too much."

"Nothing's too much for you, Prakriti," I said softly. "I just want that beautiful smile on your face."

She looked down, then back up at me, tears glimmering in her eyes. "I don't deserve you." She smiled, wiping a tear before leaning in and pressing her lips against mine. "Thank you... love you."

"Love you too." I kissed her back, and for a moment, the world seemed to fade away, leaving just the two of us standing beneath the stars.

But, as always, reality kicked in. My stomach growled, loudly enough to ruin the moment.

She burst out laughing, playfully swatting my arm. "Guess we better get back to that grill, huh?"

"Hey, kisses are great, but they won't fill our stomachs!" I teased, flipping the veggies. Prakriti refilled our glasses and then slid into my lap as we listened to the soft music, wine warming us as we watched the flames dance.

After a while, she whispered, "This night, Gaurav... it's like a dream."

"Yeah, except no samurai turtles around to wake us up." I grinned, and she chuckled, rolling her eyes at the mention of Hardy.

Morning came with a surprising visitor. Just as we were packing up, a deer and her two fawns appeared, watching us curiously from the edge of the trees. Prakriti's eyes sparkled, and without missing a beat, she started talking to them as if they understood her.

"Hey there, beautiful mama!" she cooed, holding out some bread we had left over. One of the fawns actually took a cautious step closer, nosing her hand and nibbling on the bread. I stood there, wide-eyed.

"You know they don't understand you, right?" I said, shaking my head in awe.

"Of course they do," she replied with a wink. "They're just shy." And you know what? Maybe she was right. The little ones seemed to understand her better than I ever could. They gave her one last look and disappeared back into the woods.

As we climbed back into the car, I had one more surprise up my sleeve. I pulled out some wildflowers and another little chocolate bar, handing them to her with a grin.

"Another gift?" she laughed, raising her eyebrows. "Is there anything left for the rest of the year?"

"Well, I figured, every perfect date deserves a perfect ending gift," I said, shrugging. "And hey, it's tradition now."

She shook her head, laughing, then leaned over and gave me one last kiss. "Thank you for everything, Gaurav. For tonight, for... just being you."

We drove back through the forest, the sun rising and casting a soft glow over the road, feeling like we'd just stepped out of our own little fairytale.

__Note from the Writer:__Every now and then, Gaurav and Prakriti find themselves escaping into moments that make their love story feel like something plucked straight from the pages of a dream—maybe with a little help from our friend Hardy, the self-proclaimed "samurai" turtle and unspoken guardian of the household.

This chapter was an exploration of love beyond grand gestures; it's about those seemingly small things that turn into memories. From late-night grill sessions to surprise jewelry and unexpected deer visitors, this story is woven from the threads of adventure and love, bound together by laughter, little secrets, and the playful surprises that life brings.

And yes, I may have let Gaurav squeeze in a little shout-out for BMW and Royal Enfield. Who knows, maybe Hardy has a future in advertising too!

Enjoy the journey beneath the stars, and remember to keep a little space in your life for spontaneity—it just might lead to the best moments of all.

Epilogue: Little By Little, Touch By Touch

Little by little, folks. That's how we got here, from a friendship sparked over awkward confessions, countless coffees, sunset bike rides, and, yes, even Hardy the turtle. Somehow, everything we've been through—all those wild, funny, frustrating moments—have brought us to this day. The day I finally get to put a ring on Prakriti's finger. And what a day it is!

The room is buzzing with excitement. Friends, family, cousins, kids—everyone is here, and each face holds a different memory from this journey. People are laughing, the dance floor's packed, and somewhere, I hear Destroyer—Princess, I mean—causing a bit of chaos, probably chasing poor Elizabeth the cat. It's a grand reunion of all the people (and pets) who have shaped this story.

And guess what? You're here too. The readers, the silent cheerleaders, the ones who have laughed, sighed, and (hopefully) swooned right along with us. So thanks for sticking with this story. It wouldn't be the same without you, and, hey, maybe it would've taken even longer without all those fourth-wall-breaking nudges from you folks.

The Ceremony: A Ring, a Promise

As the music softens, I look at Prakriti standing beside me, radiating grace. She's wearing a beautiful pastel lehenga, but honestly, she could be in a hoodie, and I'd still be floored. This is the woman I fell in love with—over and over again, every day. And in this moment, it's like time itself slows down, allowing us to stand still in our little universe, just for a second.

I squeeze her hand, and for once, I manage to keep my voice steady as I say, "Prakriti, as I told you before, I want to grow old with you." A smile lights up her face, and her voice is soft but clear when she replies, "And I'll be by your side, no matter what."

Hardy sits in his tank on the table, seemingly giving us a wise turtle nod as if he approves of all this mushiness. (Yes, the turtle approves. This has been turtle-verified.) Princess is barking, not-so-gracefully tangling himself in the decorations, and Elizabeth the cat lounges nearby with an unimpressed look, as cats do.

Exchange of Rings: A Forever Moment

We turn to each other, holding our rings, hands trembling slightly. And in this little silver band lies every memory, every late-night talk, every stumble and victory. I slide the ring onto her finger, feeling an overwhelming sense of calm—a peace I didn't even know I was searching for. And when Prakriti puts the ring on my finger, I can't help but grin like an absolute goofball.

In that moment, I realize: some stories don't need wild twists or epic battles to captivate. They don't need grand declarations or endless melodrama. Sometimes, love just is—quiet, steady, like the kind you find in a peaceful sunrise or a gentle river.

A Dance Floor Farewell: Fourth Wall, Who?

People are dancing, laughing, making memories. I catch sight of Koushik over by the snack table, already loading up a second plate of samosas. "Hey, don't eat everything before I get there!" I shout across the room, waving him over. He saunters over, holding up a samosa like a trophy. "Not my fault the bridegroom took too long with all that mushy stuff," he teases, grinning.

I'm tempted to lean into the fourth wall and say something cheesy, like, "No goodbyes, folks. Just see you later. Because family never really says goodbye, right?"

So, as we wind down this chapter, here's a little hint for you, dear readers: the story isn't over. There's more to come, more pages to turn. But, for now, all I want to say is thank you for joining us on this journey. For laughing, crying, and living every twist and turn. May we meet again, on another page, another story, wherever life takes us.

Until then, be well, live fully, and keep a little bit of love and adventure in your heart. You're always part of this story, even if you're not on the page.

See you in the trilogy, folks—whenever it's ready to grace your shelves.

Note From The Writer:

And here we are, at the close of *Beyond the Sunset and Stars*. What a journey it's been, both for Gaurav, Prakriti, and their beloved pet—and for you, the reader, who has been there through every twist, laugh, and heartfelt confession. This story was always a little more than just a romance or a family drama; it was a piece of a world that, somehow, you helped create just by reading along.

I've had the joy of writing Gaurav and Prakriti's story, and to bring you into their world feels like inviting you over for a cup of tea or that last plate of biryani they keep fighting over. But let's be honest, the best stories never really end, do they? There's always another dance floor, another picnic, and yes—another slice of life, chaos included.

So, thank you for reading, for laughing, and for making this journey unforgettable. The trilogy may take its time, but I promise: it will be worth the wait. For now, as Gaurav said, it's not goodbye; it's just "see you later." Until we meet again in another book, another story, keep a bit of that fourth-wall-breaking spirit with you. Here's to more love, laughter, and a little bit of chaos.

Before Sunset And Stars - The Koushik Chronicles

Alright, folks, buckle up! You've been hanging out with Gaurav and his love story for long enough, but now, it's my time to shine. Yup, you're talking to Koushik here—the best friend, college mate, and now, narrator of a brand-new saga. And yes, if you were wondering, this is the *prequel*. Think of it as "Before Sunset and Stars." Not official yet, but hey, gotta start somewhere, right?

Now, I know what you're thinking: "Koushik, we know Gaurav, the hopeless romantic; what could you possibly add to this saga?" Let me assure you—this is not your everyday rom-com. We're talking *drama*, *gym battles*, a spicy meet-cute, and yes, even a Chihuahua named Princess, who Gaurav insists on calling "Destroyer" (I still don't know why—he's an angel... most of the time).

Alright, let's set the scene: I first laid eyes on Priyanka at the gym. Now, she and I were in the same university, but you know how it is—big campus, different classes, so our paths had never crossed. But that day, I was warming up, mentally hyping myself up for another intense workout session, and there she was: lifting weights, totally focused, radiating this no-nonsense vibe. I remember thinking, *whoa, she's not here to mess around.*

Naturally, I did what any reasonable gym freak would do—I tried to play it cool. But fate had other plans, because just as I was about to finish my warm-up, in walked her ex, a guy who looked like he spent half his life at the gym...and the other half staring at himself in the mirror. You know the type.

A few days later, I brought Princess, my Chihuahua, to campus, and as fate would have it, I bumped into Priyanka outside the gym. I could see the shock in her eyes when she noticed the little guy sitting comfortably in my backpack, peeking out with his big, expressive eyes.

"Wait—this is *your* dog?" she asked, trying not to laugh. "You, Mr. Gym Buff, have a Chihuahua named Princess?"

I shrugged, giving Princess a scratch behind the ears. "What can I say? Big hearts come in small packages."

Priyanka leaned down, reaching her hand out for Princess to sniff. "Well, hello, Princess! I think Gaurav's been calling him 'Destroyer,' though. What's that about?"

I rolled my eyes. "Gaurav's got his own ideas. Something about 'small dog, big energy.' But hey, he's harmless—most of the time."

Nothing says romance like shouting over who forgot to grab the protein powder.

Note from the writer: *So, there you have it, the beginnings of Koushik's story. Sure, Gaurav has his epic sunsets and starry nights, but Koushik have got a fire-breathing Chihuahua, a gym feud, and the most incredible girl who makes every argument worth it. And if you're wondering how it all turns out...well, you'll just have to stay tuned for the rest.*

And, hey, maybe Princess will get a few more spotlight moments. After all, every love story needs a four-legged sidekick.

The Secret Society Of Shells And Shadows

Hello, hello, dear readers! It's me, Hardy, your favorite pet turtle, taking the reins while the "adults"—Gaurav and Prakriti—are off in dreamland. I know you all show them a lot of love, but let's be real: who's been here quietly watching, listening, and protecting our guy Gaurav this whole time? That's right—*me*. So, while they're snoring away, let's talk about what's actually going on.

"Hey, funny face!" I call out, casting a glance toward that little rascal, Destroyer—or should I say "Princess." It's almost painful how oblivious he is, wandering around like he owns the place.

"Are you talking to me, *turtle guy*?" he fires back, flashing that ridiculous chihuahua grin.

"Oh, please. It's *Hardy*, thank you very much. I don't need some half-pint dog with the nickname 'Princess' trying to label me," I snap, feeling my shell heat up with irritation. "And if you have any respect, keep your bladder off our guy's laptop!"

Destroyer just rolls his eyes. "Listen, I don't have time for your 'wise old turtle' lectures, buddy."

"Is that so? Well, let me clue you in. You think you're just here to chew on cables and terrorize furniture, but you're part of something bigger. Ever heard of the Secret Society?"

He tilts his head, visibly annoyed. "Secret Society? What are you talking about, old man?"

Thump. A shadow slinks into view, and out steps Elizabeth, a Persian cat with a coat so shiny it's practically its own spotlight. She's the one who introduced me to the society, a group formed to keep Gaurav safe from negative energies that seem to hover around him. "Always ready to lend a hand, Hardy," she purrs, sitting beside me and casting a cool, assessing gaze at Destroyer.

"Don't act lame, guys. This isn't Hogwarts," Destroyer scoffs, but I can tell he's curious.

"It's no joke," Elizabeth says, her voice as smooth as silk. "We're here to protect our humans from forces they can't even see, forces that feed on negativity and fear. And there's something... darker... coming. We can all feel it."

Above us, a fluttering catches our attention. It's Vegi and Rito, two lovebirds who are, quite literally, lovebirds. They look cute and all, but don't be fooled. They have a hidden power: they can fuse together into Vegito, a mighty, eagle-sized creature that could give any predator a run for its money.

Vegi speaks up, her voice light but firm. "We need all paws on deck, Destroyer. You might not think much of yourself, but even you have powers beyond what you realize."

"What are you talking about? I don't have... powers," he stammers, suddenly not so sure of himself.

"You ever notice that... well, *thing* you do at night?" I ask, giving him a sidelong look.

He looks away, scratching at his ear uncomfortably. "You mean... the werewolf thing? I thought that was just a... growth spurt or something."

"Nope," I reply, giving him a knowing nod. "You turn into a werewolf, Destroyer. And you're going to need that power when things go down."

Just then, Destroyer perks up, tail wagging slightly. "So, what are we up against?"

"Something ancient and dark," I explain, giving a serious look to each of my comrades. "We don't know exactly what it is, but we can feel it getting closer. And it's our job to make sure it doesn't reach Gaurav and Prakriti. We're the last line of defense, whether we like it or not."

Elizabeth narrows her eyes, her fur bristling slightly. "We have to train, prepare. If we're going to protect them, we need to be ready."

Vegi chirps with enthusiasm. "We'll start patrols tonight. Destroyer, I trust you'll join us?"

Destroyer straightens, giving a small but determined nod. "Count me in. I may not look like much, but I can bark like nobody's business."

Elizabeth rolls her eyes, but there's a glimmer of pride in her gaze. "Good. And try not to mark anything important next time, okay?"

Destroyer huffs. "No promises. But I'll give it my best."

Note form the Writer:_And so, dear readers, the Secret Society has spoken. A dark force may be coming, but with Destroyer's mini-werewolf might, Elizabeth's mage powers, Vegito's aerial prowess, and Hardy'sturtle wisdom (yes, that's a thing), we're ready._

But do me a favor, readers—don't tell Gaurav about this. He doesn't need to know who's really keeping him safe.This is our secret society business. Over and out.

P.S.: Keep an eye out for _Between the Sunset and Stars_, where Hardy and his friends will be back, ready to take on more hidden mysteries, wily companions, and perhaps a few secrets they've yet to discover. The adventure is far from over—trust me, this turtle has more stories to share.

What's Next In The World Of The Sunset And Stars

Thank you for joining Gaurav, Prakriti, and Hardy on their journey. This is only the beginning—there's more to discover, more adventures to unfold, and new secrets to uncover. Here's a glimpse into the series:

Before the Sunset and Stars

The story of Koushik and Priyanka, revealing how Gaurav found Hardy and the events that set everything into motion.

Beneath the Sunset and Stars

The central journey of Gaurav and Prakriti's love story, with Hardy's subtle role as their steadfast companion.

Beyond the Sunset and Stars

In this sequel, Gaurav and Prakriti face new challenges with story-bending twists that reveal just how layered their world truly is.

Between the Sunset and Stars

Follow Hardy and his band of furry and feathered friends as they protect Gaurav from unseen forces, fighting battles filled with magic and mystery. This is not a romantic comedy—but an epic tale of courage, loyalty, and friendship.

And coming soon:

A new trilogy awaits, exploring the vast universe beyond the pages you've read. Keep an eye out as these tales take shape.

Milton Keynes UK
Ingram Content Group UK Ltd.
UKHW031002261124
451618UK00006B/72